Borderlands

Borders Writers' Forum

ISBN: 979-8-4931-9801-4
Cover Design: Michael Hutchinson

CONTENTS

FOREWORD

Far tinier than a comma, invisible to the naked eye – but what havoc Covid has wrought, bereaving families, causing lasting damage to health, depriving people of their livelihoods and bringing economies to a standstill. Who would have thought, when we last produced our anthology, that our world would be so much changed?

During the past 18 months, we have hosted talks and open mic events online, with the aim of continuing to encourage and support our members in their writing lives. It's good to see that in spite of everything, creative minds have been at work. The collection of poetry and prose which follows is the result.

Our writers have explored the theme of 'Borderlands' in all its variety, as literal geographical borders, as places that keep people apart, and as places where they meet and lives touch – and of course the unique landscape and history of the Scottish Borders.

Jane Pearn
Chair, Borders Writers' Forum

THE GUN HAUNTED HER

By Susan Allen

Charlene hated the bloody thing, perched above the mantlepiece. It had been her father-in-law's. It was the gun the old man used to defend the family home and ranch from Confederate raiders. John had been barely out of his pram when he and his mother were locked in the cellar - the solid hatch hidden beneath an ancient dresser. Thankfully, his father and uncles won the day, but all Charlene could think was 'what if?' How would John and his poor mother have escaped if their menfolk had died in the skirmish?

She did something she'd never done before. She took the chair she'd just polished and put it in front of the fireplace, then reached to lift the gun from its brackets. It was heavier than she'd expected and there were cobwebs behind it. 'What the …!'

His harsh voice startled her, it made her jump – and slip.

She squeezed the trigger as she fell.

The windowpane shattered.

Her leg fractured.

John checked the gun for damage before looking down his nose at his wife.

'The gun's in one piece, little thanks to you.'

'I didn't know it was loaded … sorry … I can't stand … I think I'm going to …'

When she came to, she was strapped to the kitchen table. Dr August was in attendance.

'Not to worry, my dear. You're in safe hands. Once I've given you a shot of morphine you'll relax… and I'll re-set your leg as quickly as possible.'

Charlene's tearful eyes blinked wide open. She watched the hypodermic syringe pierce her skin and looked to her husband whose firm hands pinned down her arms. Dr August pushed and pulled. The hands tightened. Charlene screamed inwardly, then outwardly, before blackness took over.

'There, there. It was a clean break. You'll need to rest until it heals; your husband has arranged for his sister to come across to look after you.'

Dr August walked to the door with John Blake saying - 'Give it six weeks

1

and she should be able to re-commence some wifely duties, albeit she may always walk with a limp. Shame about the window, John.'

Charlene lay on a bed hurriedly installed in the corner of the room, her home for the forthcoming weeks. Through traumatised eyes she noticed the window was boarded over and, hovering in the dimness, was the overgrown shadow of the gun back in situ. She shuddered and pulled the bedsheet over her head.

'Charlene, Charlene, wake up. I've made you a drink.

Here, take this pill. The doctor says you're to take one morning and night.'

'Margaret?'

'Yes, John sent for me. You're in a bad way. You've been running a temperature and thrashing about. Here, let me prop you up.'

Margaret was thoughtful and kind. How could siblings be so different? Charlene swallowed hard. She hadn't realized she was thirsty. The pill tasted bitter.

'Could you eat a little broth? I made it fresh this morning.'

'I'll try, but just a little.'

Margaret went to the kitchen. Charlene looked around. A curtain was drawn across the boarded window. The only light came from the stairwell. She glanced at the gun.

'Margaret, do you know when the window will be repaired?'

'Better to ask me, than her,' said John.

His silhouette ominously blocked the doorway.

'Oh, hello John. I was just asking for some light.'

'That's easily sorted,' He wedged the front door wide open. 'You can close it yourself when you've had enough light.'

'I'm so sorry, John. It was an accident.'

'Best keep your hands to yourself in future - and only do as you're bid.' He turned to Margaret, 'I'll take my broth in the kitchen. You can join me. Charlene can feed herself.'

Margaret gasped. She made her sister-in-law as comfortable as she could and propped the tray across her thighs, avoiding the break lower down.

Charlene winced, her eyes the colour of steel. She'd weather this, and then...

'Do I have to keep taking these pills, Dr August?'

'It's better if you do, especially under the circumstances.'

'What circumstances are those?'

'Your husband intends sending his sister home soon.' His voice was matter of fact, although his eyes showed sympathy. It was barely three weeks, but he knew he'd already pushed his luck by insisting Margaret stay until the end of the week. He determined to increase Mrs Blake's medication to help her through.

'I understand your husband is making you crutches to help you get around. You'll need to rest your leg regularly.' He touched her hand, 'Any problems, please send for me.'

The pill took effect; Charlene drifted into oblivion.

'Margaret, thank you so much for all you've done. I hope I haven't been too demanding – look, I can now close the door on my own, using these crutches.'

Charlene dropped her legs over the side of the bed and hobbled to the door; beads of sweat dampened her hairline.

'You've been a perfect patient, Charlene. I just wish I could stay a bit longer, but …'

'But what, Margaret?' John barged the door open, catching his wife's injured leg.

'Aargh!'

'Is a man not entitled to demand his wife be mistress of her own home?' John addressed his wife.

'Next time you'll remember to stand back when I enter the room, rather than gossiping with my sister.' He looked at Margaret.

'Margaret has her own family to tend.'

'Maybe Charlene could come to me if you brought her across in the cart?' Margaret's voice was pleading. 'I'd happily make up a day bed.'

'And who'd provide my meals and keep house? No, that's not possible. This is all Charlene's doing, it's about time she made amends.' He nodded to the pair of them. 'I'll replace the glass when my wife behaves herself.'

The next two weeks were a fog. Charlene's mind was either consumed with pain or befuddled with medication. After repeated failed attempts to drag herself backwards up the stairs she was allowed to continue to use the daybed, but John would visit her each night. No words of affection, no consideration. She gritted her teeth against the onslaught as he took his conjugal rights, her head facing the wall. She didn't look at him when he grunted and rolled off.

'Stop your crying, woman. You brought this on yourself. A man has needs.' He flicked the blanket back over her, pushed his bare feet into his boots and turned towards the stairs stating: 'Tomorrow I'll repair the glass.'

Tomorrow came and finally the boarding came down. John left his wife to clean the glass. The gun seemed to grow; the cobwebs accentuated by the dust clinging to them. Charlene refused to look but she felt it looming over her as she wiped the mantlepiece. She couldn't get through the days, or nights, without her pills. Dr August called once a fortnight and brought them. He checked her leg.

'It's knitting together but I'm afraid it will be misshapen. Are you using the crutches still?'

'As much as possible, but there are times I need two hands, especially lifting the pots and pans.' Charlene instinctively pulled at her sleeves to cover the burn marks.

Dr August raised an eyebrow. John Blake was a hard man, as his father before him.

'Here, try this ointment, it will help the skin repair more smoothly.'

'I can't, John says he won't pay another cent.'

'My gift to a courageous woman.' The doctor pressed the jar into her palm.

It felt like silk on her skin. It became her morning ritual. Once John was out in the fields, she'd wash away the night's ordeal and soothe her aching leg and body with the balm. By now she had deep grooves under her armpits from the crutches, red blisters had evolved into callouses, her belly was bloated, and she struggled to tie her dress and apron.

Margaret came to visit.

'Oh, it's wonderful to see you. If I'd known, I'd have made more effort.' Charlene removed her dust-cap and pushed whisps of hair behind her ears. Her damaged leg hung against the crutch. Her body contorted.

'Are you taking your pills, Charlene?'

'I stopped yesterday. John said they made me lethargic and dopey.'

'Hmm. You sit down and take the weight off your leg, I'll put the kettle on. I've made cookies for us and thought we could sit on the veranda. It seems ages since your accident.'

'It's nearly six months.'

'It's good to see the sun shining through the window again.'

'Yes, it was a bleak winter.'

'Here, let me put a cushion under your leg. There … you look so weary.'

Charlene didn't respond. Her eyes had closed. She was asleep.

Margaret vowed to ask her husband to have a word with John. If he kept working his wife like this, he'd lose her.

'Charlene …'

Dazed, grey eyes opened.

'Here, drink this, and try one of these.'

'Thank you. You're the only one who cares.'

'I'm sure John loves you… in his own way.'

'Oh, sure… in his own way. He comes to me every night; I don't know how I'm going to cope without the pills.'

Margaret sat, shocked. Was her brother blind to Charlene's bulging belly and bowing leg?

They drank their coffee and nibbled cookies in silence.

4

'I'm sorry I'm not good company. I'm just so tired all the time.'
'I'm not surprised. Is there anything I can help with whilst I'm here?'
'Could you help me upstairs. I haven't been able to change his sheets.'
'You sit there. I'll do it.'
'No, I need to learn how to manage. If you could please help me, this one time.'

John returned home to see Charlene hopping up the stairs, one hand on Margaret's shoulder, the other on the banister. Her sister-in-law carried the crutches. He turned to face the gun.

Different pains wracked Charlene's body that night. John slid off her, she was sweating so much. He stomped away in disgust. She clutched her belly and vomited into the chamber pot. She could feel herself losing touch with her senses. She screamed. Her sanity evaporated.

'I told you to look after her, John. It's those pills. The body and mind, crave them.'
    Margaret bathed her sister-in-law's brow and chest.
'We may lose her - and the baby.'
'What? How do you know? About the child.'
'I use my eyes. She's carrying high, it's likely a boy.'
    John looked at his wife, at her belly, her saturated bed.
'Do everything you can to save them. Shall I get more pills from Dr August?'
'Definitely not – they've done enough damage. I'll do my best. It would help if she could have privacy, maybe use the bedroom upstairs… could you manage down here for a while? Then I could camp next to her and tend her day and night, until…'
    'Until what?'
'Until she comes back from the brink, God willing.'
    John carried his wife upstairs before sitting in the rocker downstairs, in the shadow of the gun, waiting. The screaming and groaning continued night and day, day and night, until all was silent. Then he worried. He tapped on the bedroom door.
    'Come in, John.'
'She looks …' he swallowed, 'lifeless.'
'Not quite, she's still breathing but exhausted. She'll need help for the foreseeable future. I'll send Marnie across.'

Marnie was a mature black woman, an emancipated slave – just. The borderlands benefited from cheap labour. John left the trundle next to Charlene's bed for her.

'I expect you to keep house, feed me and make sure the child is born. Is that clear?'

'Yes, Sir.' Marnie bobbed a curtsy.

The days passed and Charlene grew stronger. Marnie stayed. John was taking no chances – he wanted this son.

'Did you escape the South, Marnie?'

'Yes, Mrs Charlene. Mrs Margaret, she takes me in, feeds me and lets me sleep in the house. She even pays me to "do" for her and says she'll pay me to "do" for you, too.'

'She's a good woman, Marlene. There's you - spent years as a slave, now free. And there's me. Born free - now married into slavery for the rest of my days.' Charlene's voice cracked.

'I thought maybe I'd sit you on the veranda today, the weather's mild and I could watch you from the vegetable plot. I need herbs for a tonic.'

'Of course – I'd like that, the fresh air.'

Charlene took the tonic and started to blossom. She could feel her baby kicking.

John watched from a distance, scowling. He started to lose weight. One morning he didn't get up. Dr August was called.

'Well, John. This is a sorry state-of-affairs. I can't put my finger on exactly what the problem is, but bed rest and these should help.' He left John morphine pills.

Marnie fed John home-made broth seasoned with herbs but still he grew weaker. His strength seemed to ebb and transfer to Charlene and the baby.

Margaret came to visit.

'Oh, John. Is there anything I can do?'

'Leave me alone, for one thing. I'm fed up with you goddam women fussing around.'

His eyes glared ferociously from sunken sockets. He took more pills.

The broth went untouched.

Charlene kept her distance.

Marnie did what she could – she made him a tonic too.

The night Charlene went into labour the wind howled and the shutters rattled.

'Do you hear that? There's someone out there. It's those bloody Confederates come to take our ranch. I'll stop them.'

'John, no, the baby's coming!'

'That's women's work.'

He thrust his feet into his boots, grabbed his father's gun and dived into the darkness in nothing but his undergarments. They heard gunshot.

6

'I can't see a thing, can you Marnie?'

'No Mrs, it's pitch black out there. I'm surprised the master can see anything.'

'I don't think he can. I think it's all in his head, like it was in mine - for a while.'

The pangs took over. His child was ready for this world.

Dawn came. Their daughter was born.

Marnie searched the outbuildings and fields. There was no sign of John, or interlopers. The gun lay near the well. She ran for help. Thank goodness she'd brought extra water into the house for the birth.

He was laid to rest next to his father. Charlene insisted the gun be buried with him.

Margaret held the babe. John's crippled widow dropped soil onto his coffin, and Marnie scattered herbs.

Two weeks later Marnie sang in the kitchen as she prepared Mrs Charlene's tonic. Charlene rocked and hummed a lullaby.

'There'll be no gun to ruin your life, my precious daughter.'

'And there's no man to ruin yours, Mrs Charlene.'

The radiant mother smiled.

'I'm glad you decided to stay, Marnie.'

'Mrs Margaret is happy I did, too.'

The chimney breast is free of cobwebs. A vase of bright meadow flowers stands on the mantlepiece.

CROSSING OVER

By Rosalyn M Anderson

Alfred Lord Tennyson was neither Scottish nor a Borderer but held the honour of UK Poet Laureate for 42 years and was the first British citizen to be awarded a peerage for writing. These are worthy facts for sharing but it is his epic poem, Crossing The Bar, later set to music, which brings a Border connection – well for me anyway! Written, allegedly, on a boat on the Solent, perhaps on a very rough crossing, he spoke of the journey we all ultimately make, between life and death and I suggest that anyone travelling north or south over the Carter Bar on a bad weather day, could be forgiven for thinking his poem may have been written right there!

The Carter Bar is a noted tourist destination, at the head of the Redesdale Valley in Northumberland, marking the boundary between Scotland and England. It is well known for extremes of weather, catching many folk off-guard, especially in the deep winter months. The inhospitable territory allows no refuge and with no options for emergency accommodation for many miles. If you manage to summit the peak through the deep snow and progress northwards away from The Cheviots and down to the lower-lying Jed Water Valley, your journey can feel like your last one, as your tyres slip and slide whilst your heart misses a beat for all the wrong reasons.

My advice to the reader is therefore to make the momentous border crossing on the best weather day possible and take your time; time to drink in the stunning vista as the Scottish Borders appears in all its glory. On a bright sunny day, your heart will race as the hills, valleys and green hues of diverse forestry open up before you, all ripe for exploring to reveal the ruined abbeys, castles and peel towers, all with their own rich history.

Whether or not the Carter Bar piper is offering a 'Welcome to Scotland' medley, as you pause you may feel a sense of the history of the land on which you stand and where so many bodies are buried.

The long-gone hamlet of Carter Bar bore witness to the many arguments and alleged 'truces' made close to this spot. The lowland clans did not forget the attempts at 'pacification of the Borders' by King James VI (of Scotland), which had inflamed loyalties with tragic results. During the bloody border feuds of the Killing Times of the late 17th century, the religious beliefs of Charles II and their imposition on the Scottish people, led to a truly vicious period of history, hot on the heels of the turbulent reiving times. The Border Reiving had become an accepted horror from the 13th century onwards, when individuals could not refuse the summons to join the 'hot trod' at an appointed hour, to plunder cattle and burn farmsteads. Many other dreadful deeds were performed by Scots and English on both sides of the border and the names of the Reivers live on in the Armstrongs, Scotts, Elliots and Kers and a mis-placed consonant can cause old rivalries to re-surface.

Many Border Ballads, kept alive by traditional singers in the area today, vividly capture these awful times and were collected and published by Sir Walter Scott in his Minstrelsy of the Borders. It was a much earlier Sir Walter Scott (of Branxholme), who, in the 16th century, as an infamous Reiver, wreaked considerable havoc across the countryside claiming land, goods and chattels for his own. He is remembered particularly for his part in the freeing of Kinmont Willie Armstrong, another cattle-stealing brigand, who was detained in Carlisle Castle. His unleashing by his band of followers is duly commemorated in a ballad, and inevitably this paints a very different picture from the tour guides of Carlisle.

Strong geographical loyalties have persisted through the centuries and unseen 'borders' are marked and celebrated during the annual Common Ridings. These are almost unique to the Scottish Borders region though a few exist in neighbouring parts of Scotland. Very different ceremonies to 'beat the bounds' also occur across the UK. Each Scottish Border border settlement has their very own individual identity, linked not only to their history, but most importantly, to their location. Many of the towns are located alongside water which powered the textile mills of the past. The Tweed, Teviot and Jed and Gala Waters are all remembered in the Common Riding songs. Most of these annual festivals feature vast numbers of riders on horseback, with 'ex pats' returning from far and wide to join the events of the week. Hawick's Common Riding involves the unique spectacle of horses racing high above the town on a course dating from the mid-19th century, where even watching the races is not for the faint-hearted. Many of the riders have been partaking of rum and milk since the very early hours and slippage in the saddle is a definite risk!

Selkirk's particular celebration is specifically linked to the Battle of Flodden on Northumbrian soil and the return of the lone Selkirk soldier, Fletcher, bearing the flag of an English troop. The haunting lament, with the official title, 'The Floo'ers o' the Forest', (with the Floo'ers or Flowers being the young men struck down in their prime at the Battle) exists in at least two forms, with 'The Liltin' version having been written by Jean Elliot, a descendant of the famous Border Reiving clan from the Liddesdale area.

It is Jedburgh's Common Riding which includes a cavalcade of riders travelling from the town south to The Carter Bar, not an easy ride even in summer, where the assembled gathering remember one of the last significant border battles and the subject of another Border ballad, called 'The Raid of the Redeswire.'

If only the Carter Bar could speak or sing us tales of those who have passed across the summit, whether transported or on foot. as they swapped one country for another, often temporarily. The Romans crossed the Bar as they sought to extend their Empire and saw ahead of them The Three Hills of Eildon, leading them onward to found Trimontium, their Border base which lasted for at least one hundred years and where they left a rich legacy of historical artefacts buried deep in the clay for excited archaeologists to research for The Trimonitium Trust and Museum.

Many travellers now arrive to walk one of the many long-distance paths which traverse the region, crossing the rolling hills of the borders so wonderfully commemorated in song in the 1960s by the late Matt McGinn. He had travelled widely in his folk-singing career but felt the beauty of the border hills could not be beaten. His moving chorus carries the sentiments of many and I can think of no better way to end than with his tribute to this special place, one of the many gems of Scotland:

'When I die, bury me low
Where I can hear the bonnie Tweed flow
A sweeter place I never did know
Than the rolling hills o' the Borders.'

Words by Matt McGinn, copyright Janetta Music

CROSSING THE BORDER

By Antoine d'Y Bisset

The afternoon light slanted through the tall sash windows and the colours in the Persian carpet glowed like a stained glass window.

A boy was sitting in the light. He was sitting on a small wooden box which had worn paintings of planes and sailing ships on the sides. He was about nine years old. He was dressed in short trousers and a woollen T-shirt.

In front of him on the carpet was a small army of painted soldiers; somewhat mixed up; some in red uniforms and some in blue; some on horseback with swords or lances and moveable arms. The others were infantry fixed in positions of imminent violence, rifles at the ready and bayonets fixed. Many of the soldiers were veterans of fierce battles; some were missing arms, or had broken lances and stumps of swords. A couple of the horses had lost a leg and could only hobble into battle.

The coloured paint was worn and chipped and where it was missing entirely, a dull grey metal showed.

A big green cannon sat near the middle of the carpet with one large wooden cannon ball next to it.

The boy, whose name was David, was speaking to his soldiers, as he divided them into two groups, the Reds and the Blues.

He was preparing for a battle between the two armies. The Blues, fewer in number, were the army of the High People and the Reds were the army of the Folk.

David arranged the Blues in a crescent across a corner. They had crossed the border just at dawn and were preparing to attack from High Corner.

The Reds were formed into sections, tight groups of infantry and a column of lancers. Behind them, in the central medallion of the carpet, the cannon had been placed.

The heavy wooden ball was dropped down the barrel and the cannon was loaded, to make ready to fire.

David readied the cannon by pulling back on a spring-loaded lever and notched it in place. A flick of the finger would release the lever and the spring would propel the cannon ball towards the enemy.

The long barrel pointed toward the Blues in the High Corner.

Troops on both sides marched and marshalled, backwards and forwards. General David, commander of the High Army of the Blues was preparing to launch an attack against Commandant David, chief of the Army of the Red Folk.

He was continually reviewing positions, moving squadrons and

11

companies from one position to another seeking a perfect attacking opportunity for the Blues and a fierce counter-attack for the Reds. This time, David was sure the Reds' cannon would assure victory for the Reds, no matter how many were lost to the superior training and determination of the smaller number of Blues.

He fired the cannon. A practice round, it flew over the army of the Blues, clattering off the wall and rattling on the wooden floor beyond the bounds of the carpet.

There was the sound of feet on the staircase. Hard shoes clicked on the parquet floor in the hall. Miss Stephens stood in the open doorway. David's nanny.

The boy resented her. He was too big for a nanny. He could dress himself, tie his shoelaces and command armies. Yet he had to do whatever Miss Stephens told him.

She looked down at him, her hands on her hips. She did not smile.

'Listen to me.'

David looked up. He saw no softness in her face.

'I need you to keep quiet and not run around.' She paused.

'Do you understand?'

David nodded reluctantly.

'Good! Well, Master David, you will please stay in this room and play quietly. You will not depart from this carpet. There is the border.'

Her black polished shoe moved over the edge of the woollen carpet and touched the border, a narrow double stripe decorated with symbolic roses.

'This border goes all the way round. You will not cross it until I tell you that you may. I will come back. I will be watching and I will be listening. Please stay inside the border. If you cross the border I will do something terrible. Is that clear?'

David again nodded. 'Yes, Nanny Stephens.'

The nanny looked into David's face with an unbending gaze. He dropped his eyes. The black shoe drew back to the polished hardwood floor.

With a clack of her heels, the nanny turned, left the room, and crossed the hall into the lounge diagonally opposite.

She sat on the settee. David could only see her hand on the end of the armrest and her trousered leg and her crossed ankles as she stretched her legs a little.

From her position she could not see him at all.

In the quiet of the house, where the silence was measured by the gentle ticking of the mantel clock she would be able to hear every cough, every sniffle, every command given to the armies of the Red and Blue.

David returned to his martial dispositions. The Blues were outnumbered, but their cause was just. The Reds, powerful and arrogant, had captured the Princess Rowangold and had demanded a ransom.

The Blues had crossed the border this very morning. They had come silently, their horses' hooves covered in sackcloth to deaden the noise. Now they were in the corner, preparing to rescue their beloved princess or die in the attempt.

David moved the Blue Hussars into the centre of their line. They would charge the guns.

Behind them the Blues' infantry took their positions ready to advance as soon as the cavalry trumpets announced the attack.

Commandant David advanced the wings of the Red infantry, on the left the Grenadiers, and on the right the Red Guards. The Blues would have to advance between them, straight at the Reds' artillery.

The Red Lancers were being held back to act as reinforcements when required.

A brief, quiet, trumpet call signalled the start of the slow deliberate advance of the Hussars.

It was time to load the guns.

David sighed. He had fired the only cannon ball before nanny had entered. It was now in the corner of the room, in the angle of two walls, and seven feet from the closest part of the carpet.

David knew it was seven feet because he had measured everything the previous week. Before he became a Commander of Armies he had been a Builder.

He could not reach the wooden ball without crossing the forbidden border. Maybe he could lasso it with string? There was no string. Perhaps he could dislodge it with a garden cane? He looked across the room. There was a garden cane in the big pot with the dragon tree, but it too was out of reach.

Perhaps he could make a rope out of his clothes as he had done when he had escaped from the pirate ship of Black Jack Tregenza the previous week?

He was wearing a T-shirt and shorts. Even if he used his socks and underpants it was not going to work.

The only solution was to crawl very quietly, or very quickly, to the corner and bring back the ball.

He was afraid of 'something terrible'.

He could continue the battle without using the cannon. If he did, the Blues, outnumbered though they were, would cut through the Reds and claim victory.

That would be too easy. Nor would it be as exciting.

He sat still. He was thinking. His eyes roamed around the room for something that might help him. There was nothing on the carpet. The straight-backed chairs and polished furniture were arranged around the walls of the big room. Angled buttresses of sunlight came through the sash windows, creating columns of dark shadow.

David took off his sandals. If he threw one into the corner it could rebound on the ball and send it back to the edge of the carpet. Perhaps. It would surely make enough noise to be heard by nanny.

He looked across the hall through the open doors. Nanny was still sitting in the same place on the sofa.

As he looked, he heard the ringing of the telephone. It rang and rang. At last nanny arose from the sofa, her dark head and glasses coming into view as she drew in her legs as she got to her feet.

She made no sound as she crossed the thick lounge carpet to the telephone table on the opposite side of the room. The telephone continued to ring, and was cut off in mid ring as nanny picked up the handset.

'Swinton 643,' she said, sounding slightly crisp and cross. Then her voice changed. She spoke more gently, drawing out her vowels, 'Oh, it's you …'

Her voice dropped to a murmur and David could no longer make out the words.

David considered his feet, the thin cotton socks with the hedgehog pattern. If Nanny Stephens was talking on the telephone out of sight, he could maybe move quickly and quietly, retrieve the ball and be back on the carpet without making a sound, without being seen.

That is if he were both quick and quiet. If he were brave enough.

He had been very brave when he had been fighting in the Crusades. But this was different. He could forget the infidels and they would vanish for as long as he wished, until the moment when he returned to the Crusades.

But this was different. Nanny Stephens lived in his house. He could not make Nanny Stephens vanish.

David stood up. The carpet was soft under his feet. He stepped forward. There was no sound. He moved quietly to the edge of the carpet, his toes on the floral strip of the border only a few inches from the polished wooden floor. The parquet stretched across the room, like a sea, to where the wooden ball floated in the corner like a lost sailor in a foreign ocean.

He could cross that sea, stepping out across it like a colossus come to life. He could rescue the lost sailor and bring him safe to shore.

But he was afraid. Nanny Stephens could return at any time, now or very soon. Her voice could still be heard murmuring softly from time to time, in response to the other party.

How long would the call last?

Long enough to dash across the Sea of Atlantis, catch up the ball and return to the carpet, to the land of safety in a hostile sea?

A sudden noise from the lounge gave David a start, dragging him back from his imaginings into an anxious reality. Nanny Stephens had given a short loud laugh. David sighed. She was still on the phone. Time was passing.

He twiddled his toes inside his socks. The hedgehogs wriggled. He knew that time was passing and when nanny returned from the lounge, his chance to retrieve the cannon ball would be gone. The battle would not take place and the princess would continue to remain a prisoner.

As his thoughts turned to the running out of time he could hear, almost insistently, the ticking of the clock. Had it always been so loud? He'd never really noticed it before even though it had always been there, ticking, ticking. On the hour it would strike. He looked up at the mantelpiece. The minute hand was almost at three. The second hand moved in almost imperceptible tiny stutters.

If he made a dash when the clock struck, the gong-like sounds would drown out any   noise he made. He shivered.

Blood pounded in his head, suddenly hot. If not now ...

He crouched at the edge, waiting like a runner for the crack of the starter's pistol.

Bong! He was off. He ran across to the corner, his hand already extended to catch up the ball. As he tried to slow down, his feet slipped, smooth socks sliding on the waxed wood. His feet slid into the corner and he sat down with a bump. Bong! The clock struck again. It rang in his head as he started to get up. He took up the ball in his hand and crouched on all fours, like a little dog, he turned to go back to the carpet.

Black shoes and silk stockings appeared under his nose. He looked up. The legs in black tailored trousers were topped by a red blouse. Nanny Stephens. She looked down on him as a man might regard an ant.

'Stand up,' she said.

David got unsteadily to his feet, his socks slip-sliding on the floor.

'Look at me,' said Nanny Stephens. 'Tell me if you crossed the border. Did you?'

'Yes,' whispered David, his voice hoarse, his mouth suddenly dry.

'Yes, you did,' said Nanny Stephens. 'You know what happens now.'

'Something terrible,' said David, his voice almost inaudible.

'Quite so. Now put your soldiers back in the box and give them all to me.'

David gathered together his armies, Reds and Blues. He put them carefully back into the wooden toy box, with the big cannon and the big wooden cannon ball. He gently closed the box, hooked the catch and handed the box up to nanny. The terrible thing had happened. His toys were gone. The princess would be a prisoner until another day.

'Good,' said Nanny Stephens, 'they are all now prisoners of war and will be held in Nannya until I think you deserve their release. Now please go and read a book. Tea with scones and jam will be in an hour.'

THE YOUNG CHARLIE FARR

By Antoine d'Y Bisset

O young Charlie Farr rade oot o' the West.

Through a' the wide Border his Harley was best.

Save his sharp quiff, he weapons had none.

He revved his bike's engine and soon 'did the ton'.

Sae frequent in drink and fuddled in bar,

there wiz nary an Angel like fat Charlie Farr.

He stopped no fur red light, he braked no fur bends,

he roared through the hairpins, laying bike on its ends.

Sae boldly he swaggered, steppin' up tae her hoose.

He swung his crash helmet, his leathers were loose.

He tugged at his beard, he jabbed at the bell,

there wur noises inside, sae loud he could tell.

Bride's faither appeared, he wiz haudin' a can,

Said, 'Bella's no here, she's awa wi' her man

Tae far Caribbean, so they'll baith hae a tan.

They were merrit last month withoot ony fuss

And left fur the airport in a shiny green bus.

If ye'd been a sight quicker and no sic a ninny

She'd no gaun an' merrit thon bam fae Barlinnie.'

Oor boy was fair flummoxed, he hudnae a thought

That Bella would ditch him - true love cam tae naught.

It's slowly sunk in, he's cam ower a' sad,

So mebbe, aye surely, he'd mooch a wee nip fae her dad?

CROSSING THE LINE

By Hayley Emberey

'It smells rank in here. The stench reminds me of neglected soldiers being prepared for that dreadful war.' Carl Klopp bent over, solemnity scarring his face. He picked a rusty old children's tricycle from beneath the rubble. 'Nobody really cared then. I suppose at least some poor child may have had some enjoyment peddling around on this unkempt terrain.'

'What's this?' Carl's long-lost comrade, Hamish Cameron, rustled a muddy scrap of card betwixt his fingertips. Brushing the morsels of dirt to one side, he realised he might have an exciting valuable prized possession within his grasp. He read:

'Dear Mama. As this is the only way to contact you, I hope you get this. Life is rough here. The camp grows bigger every day as more German prisoners are brought in from across the border. They get paraded around. Almost full at 4000 now. So, there is even less food to eat. Am trying to keep warm but we only get one thin blanket each. Walked to Hawick the other day to get this postcard for you. Am looking after Billy, don't worry. I hope this wretched war is over soon. The training here was bleak, but this reality is hell. Miss you. All my love always, Ernest.

Stobs Camp, 22nd August 1916.'

Hamish cleared his throat, a tear snailed down his left cheek. He could only just decipher a picture of Hawick town centre on the back. No stamp was visible. The address read:

Mrs Mavis McTavish
23, Glenmore Close
Fife

'It's a fair trek into town from here. Do you remember that old newspaper article about the troops who were training here when it was a military camp, were allowed a rare parade into Hawick? At least they were appreciated by the crowds. That was before the camp became a POW camp.' Carl nodded, he remembered.

He then pointed to the one remaining original building. A child's shoe lay in the dirt on the floor outside a smashed window of the old washroom. Buckles. The old-fashioned shoe buckle was still intact. A small, yellow, hard-cased ladies' suitcase sat resting. Were it to be opened, whisperings of past memories, some precious, some haunting, would no doubt be revealed. Carl's eyes roamed around the other derelict buildings. He became transfixed, drawn by a large hut with the number 27 on a plaque above a warped, wooden door. He peered tentatively in through the window, for fear of a bat or moth or bird, one of which might mistake him for an intruder. Lying on the threadbare doormat, was a set of ripped, scuffed pages from an old book. Carl put his hand through a hole in the door and reached out for it. One or two corners of the pages disintegrated into dust. As he rose to his feet, he looked inquisitively at the content. A deep sigh poured from his lips, 'An old love story. Definitely an adult's book, judging by the content! Captain Samuel Watson and a Lady Penelope Brodie. Published in 1902. We'll keep that.'

Hamish paused, a sense of relief shone out through his eyes. 'So they had some means of escape into a better world I suppose. Nothing beats a good love story when you are only in the company of men all day with such a desolate conflict going on all around you. How many times will it take in history, before humanity stop crossing the line?' Carl shook his head, placed his right hand on his heart, gently caressed his chest. A depth of despair and sorrow momentarily engulfed his entire being as though his soul was so exhausted by what he could feel and imagine his ancestors must have endured. Pulling himself together, he softly spoke, 'So, when the war ended, they released the German prisoners back across the border, a lot of whom resided in the U.K. anyway. This camp would have been abandoned as fast as a hummingbird flaps its wings or zebras run from a pack of hyenas. Then it was just left to rack and ruin.' Silence filled the space between them. A fog began to sink below the grey array of heavy rain clouds. Hamish raised his right arm, punched the air and exclaimed 'We're going to Lindisfarne!'

The drive over the rickety planks disturbed the anatomies of the two senior comrades as they crossed the sea to what was originally called Lindisfarne, now known as Holy Island. The sun beamed down on the truck bonnet as it was parked up abruptly. Hamish stroked his beard and sniffed the sea air. 'What a beautiful spot. Must have been terrifying though being attacked for the first time by those merciless, Vikings.' The two comrades got out of the truck and walked across the gravel towards the remains of the castle. Quite a long road submerged in pink lupins. Carl and Hamish embraced the well-known view across the sea to Bamburgh Castle. Carl muttered, 'Well, we might be in England but it was Oswald, the

Northumbrian King who summoned Aidan from Iona in 635, off the south-west coast of Scotland to be bishop of his kingdom, where he founded the monastery to spread Christianity.'

'So, who is St. Cuthbert then?' Hamish began feeling inadequate.

'St. Cuthbert was the Saint now buried in Durham Cathedral. The monks apparently opened up his tomb eleven years after his death and he had not decayed, proving he was incorrupt, much to the annoyance of those averse to his purity and saintliness in life. His body got elevated into a shrine and miracles there were soon reported. In death, he attracted grants of land and wealth from the likes of the Scottish Kings and the Borderers. Prior to then, the Vikings came in and raided Lindisfarne on 8th June 793.' Carl shuddered at the thought, 'those Vikings may have been brutal but they had smart selfish intentions to find new land to farm and grow crops. Scandinavia was too cold. Hey, Hamish, come and look at this.' Hamish shuffled closer to see what his elder, highly informed, intelligent comrade had to show him. Hamish had known Carl for a long time, but he hadn't seen this side of him before. 'It's hard to believe this actual place was where the first Viking raid happened in the whole of Western Europe. Feels sort of eerie. The soft, pacifying monks were much more of an easy target than the warrior Picts across the border. That's why the Vikings ended up crossing the border further south causing such devastation.' He paused for a moment whilst such images sank in. 'Anyway, let's go and take a look at St. Mary's Church?'

With Hamish's approval, Carl led the way into the grounds of the churchyard. It was from the church that the surviving monks, amidst the Viking attacks, managed to salvage some of the treasures, the tomb of St. Cuthbert and fled south. The statue of St.Aidan stood tall, praying his message of peace, humbleness, salvation, forgiveness and service to those in need. Carl and Hamish wandered graciously as a cloud among the graves, until a particular stone caught Hamish's eye. 'Carl, look at this. I think it shows the name, 'Ernest Mc Tavish. Died 795AD. Aged 35 years. God rest his soul. Blessed are those loyal to St.Cuthbert.' Can you believe it? He keeps popping up.' Hamish bore a wry, meaningful smile for the first time in a long time. Stroking his beard, he delighted in stating 'This Ernest chap has coincidentally been around a lot longer than we think. '

The fiery, red stone of the formidable military fortress of Tantallon Castle stood tall against the skyline. Whilst flocks of seabirds nested on the famous protruding rock out at sea, no one could doubt the despair and fear those resident in the castle must have felt centuries ago as the castle went under siege on at least three occasions. As the two comrades approached along the pathway, even Carl and Hamish felt a tingling presence of deep-rooted history and bloodthirsty battles pass through their veins. The Douglases, one of Scotland's mightiest medieval families, built the monstrosity of a castle in a French chateau style for William Douglas, 1st Earl of Douglas in the 1350's. Carl and Hamish's jaws dropped open as they arrived at the Mid Tower. Carl looked around at the vastness in front of him and with a hint of sarcasm, said, 'So this is what the English did in those bloody, violent years of constant crossing the border to take over land and castles. How ironic, Tantallon's main purpose was simply to provide a comfortable residence for a wealthy and powerful nobleman, his family and staff. It must have been a wonderful place in its heyday anyway, before Cromwell ordered Monck to invade in 1650.'

'Yes, because the English were on a mission to destroy any Scottish support for Charles II having just cut off the head of Charles I!' Hamish grunted disgruntled. Carl continued, 'Sorry, but how did they manage to cause so much devastation? Look at the derelict state of the masonry wall beside the outer gate and the shattered stumps of the Douglas Tower and East Tower. That could only be caused due to the size and number of guns in Monck's army.'

'So you just answered your own question then', Hamish was slightly waning with a touch of envy at his comrade's historical prowess so he had to have a sarcastic jibe. Carl spoke again with such awe and wonder at the thought of how many people had entered in and out of those walls. 'A lot of people passed through these gates over the years. Famous ones, Mary Queen of Scots, Queen Victoria.' Hamish interrupted, 'Yes, the English came up centuries later to try to make amends for the dreadful damage they had caused in the past. They crossed the border with a slightly better intention than before, although of course they had to be in control of what happened to this place in the future! They still haven't ever got it back to its former glory. I doubt if they ever will!' Carl looked inquisitively at his dear friend, 'Hmm. I get the feeling you're a very patriotic Scot mate!' Hamish decided there was no need to comment on such an obvious answer. He swiftly moved towards the dovecote where they used to house over 1000 pigeons, eaten before they even had the chance to fly. Carl called out after him, 'Hey, Hamish! What's up?'

'I just need some space, Carl. Sorry.' Hamish turned away, carried on walking, his shoulders slightly hunched, his head bowed. He shuffled his boots along the grass kicking a random stone out of the way. He felt very overwhelmed, confused about how a race could knowingly drive its own kind to the point of madness and slaughter, defying the old commandments, thou shalt not kill, thou shalt not steal! How he wished it was all just a horrible nightmare. As Hamish arrived at the dovecote he read the small placard outside. In the distance he could hear the scrunching sound of approaching footsteps. He turned around thinking perhaps Carl was not willing to give him a bit of space, but he did not recognise the man standing there now in front of him. 'Hello, sir.' Hamish raised his head, pushed his shoulders back, cleared his throat and stuttered a few words, feeling a sense of uneasiness in case he was not allowed to be at the dovecote. 'Hello, sir. Sorry. Am I not supposed to be here?'

The ruddy faced gentleman wore a hard helmet, a blue overall and exuded a warm smile. 'No, no, no. Don't worry. You're allowed to be here. We are sorting the loose masonry in the main castle area which can obviously be a danger to visitors.'

'I understand. Hence the funny hat!'

'Yes.' The two gentlemen exchanged a mutual grin. 'So, how long have you been working here?' Hamish was now over his momentary need to have some space.

'A couple of weeks but I know the site pretty well. My ancestors were related to the Douglas family. Cousins, I think. Distant cousins. So some of my ancestors would probably have been firing bullets from up there trying to defend the fortress! 'Doon Doon Tantalloon' the enemy used to chant, beating their drums. What about Lindisfarne though, those wild Vikings, or the First World War at those POW camps. I think one of them was a stone mason, Archibald and the other, Margaret, a cook.'

'Oh, that's interesting. We have stone masons in our family as well as carpenters.' As they continued their conversation, two other gentlemen appeared. Hamish was pleased to see Carl again, a familiar face. He was beginning to feel guilty about walking away from his old friend. Hamish then noticed his new acquaintance seemed to recognise the other gentleman approaching who was also wearing a hard hat. 'Hello bro. How are you doing?' Both gentlemen reached out to shake each other's hands. They obviously knew each other very well. 'Oh, let me introduce you.' The gentleman who had been talking to Hamish turned to his comrade and presented 'so this is Billy.'

Hamish put out his hand to shake Billy's hand, 'pleased to meet you, Billy.'

Billy replied 'Likewise, and you are?'

Hamish introduced himself. 'My name is Hamish Cameron and this is my old comrade, Carl Klopp.' They exchanged further handshakes. Then the last gentleman in the group said 'and my name is Ernest McTavish.

IN NOT SO SPLENDID ISOLATION*

By Michael Fenty

It's a surreal world we are living in. Social isolation, communication by internet, conversations across the width of a road. This pestilence has changed the way we live, possibly for ever.

We are lucky, living in a small village in the country. We can walk for miles in our permitted exercise time without seeing a soul and yet the spring continues to burst out in the gardens and woods unaware of our human restrictions. Unthinking about our problems, the rest of the planet just gets on with what it has always done.

Violets bloom on a bank, a buzzard screams in the sky, the summer visitors arrive, the warblers and the swallows come back to their old haunts, the badgers seek new setts, oblivious of us.

Our ancient village of Coldingham has seen it all before. There is a plague stone near the edge of the village. Almost four hundred years ago, the inhabitants of Northfield, then a small hamlet, now a large farm, were struck by an outbreak of plague and quarantined. People didn't really understand the germ theory but they knew that contact spread the contagion so they filled the basin -like hollow in the top of the stone with vinegar and the folk from Northfield would put their coins in the vinegar to buy food.

Today, the local butcher brought eggs, fresh vegetables and fruit to the doorstep and we left the money for him in an envelope. Plus ca change! Yet people are risking their lives to minister to the sick, to care for the vulnerable, and to treat and save the seriously afflicted.

We appreciate them now, but will we continue to do so when the plague is defeated or will we go back to idolising vacuous 'personalities', sports persons and commentators, game show hosts and all their associated trivia and lavishing vast sums upon them when their contribution is, as we have discovered, at best borderline and mostly unnecessary. We shall see.

* Written in April 2020

IN THE FOOTSTEPS OF ROBBIE BURNS

By Vee Freir

the plaque half-way on Coldstream bridge

proclaims historic significance

Robbie Burns crossed here

knelt and prayed

for peace and health

of Scotia's countrymen

these trees, reaching out

over the nature-made border

were they here, to watch that moment?

did he, like me, caress the stones?

look back at Scotland's border town

enhanced by sun on the Tweed?

Borderland Sanctuary

By Pamela Gordon

I'll rest here among these rocky outcrops until dusk. Then I'll follow the rough path down the escarpment, through the bracken, until I reach the cover of the trees. I dare not risk that descent in the dark, with the sheer drop on one side where the track curves round the top of the ravine. I'll just have to pray my nondescript clothes merge into the background as night falls.

I've come so far. I have no choice but to take the risk and venture onto that treacherous terrain. It's the last hurdle. I must have a chance. The guards in the watchtower below the crest of the mountain range have a wide area to cover. They're bound to concentrate on the main footpath down to the bend in the river, beyond where the cliff juts out. Along that stretch of riverbank some of their comrades patrol on foot to pick off rash would-be migrants who chance their luck on the old tourist track. It's a much easier route – which makes it obvious. That's where Georg and his family came to grief … but I won't let myself think of them or what might have been.

I must aim for the inlet where the ravine cuts into the bank and the sheer cliff cuts it off from the rest of the riverside. From there I can go straight into the water, push off from the nearest rock and try to glide, head down, as far as I can. I'm not the fastest swimmer. I'd never win a race. But I am quite strong and I know how the current flows. I know where I should be able to come ashore. If I can reach the river, I'll be all right. Surely I'll be all right? I know some victims have been shot in the water. It would be difficult to prove where exactly they were when the gun was fired, which side of the invisible line along the centre of the churning stream. Our cautious neighbours on the far bank don't want a diplomatic incident. They've left an open strip of borderland beside the river, a cordon sanitaire, for refugees to stumble across to reach the reception centre. They're ready to accept those who make it to the building, to claim asylum, but they won't intervene outside the undisputed bounds of their territory, especially not between another sovereign state and its citizens. Knowing what we do, who can blame them?

It's funny to think that in the old days boatloads of visitors came to moor at the jetty at the foot of the tourist track, which the guards demolished after the civil war started. People from all over the world came ashore and climbed to the waterfall higher up the ravine, so they could admire the view and gawp at the power of nature. It also meant they'd set foot in another country for an hour or two – another tick to increase their tally – a country they'd regard as a bit exotic, still rather authoritarian but gradually opening up to the wider world. So we thought. Then came the coup and the counter-coup and neighbour turned against neighbour in a way I couldn't have imagined, growing up here in assumed security, perceived civilization, blinkered ignorance. Ancient hostilities, long suppressed, erupted. Fear of 'the Other' burgeoned and fostered atrocities. Throats were cut and rape was weaponised, babies butchered, grandmothers savaged ...

No, I won't dwell on those horrors. I have to believe this is an aberration which will pass, a trauma convulsing my country which will end. But I daren't stay to find out, not now my writings have been proscribed. I must focus on the different life which I can experience: over there across the river, over the border. That's what I must think of, concentrate my mind on: where there is hope. I'll pretend I'm preparing an academic treatise on the subject. After all, it's what I used to teach before I was banned. I know all the theory, the history and geography in many places. I'll recite the introductory lecture in my head – a bird's eye view of a multifaceted subject, albeit focused just on Europe.

'Border' is a hard-edged word conjuring pictures of lines on a map, documentation, Border checks, customs posts. More seriously borders can involve walls to keep out the unwelcome, detention centres, lookout posts and sharp-shooters. Borders, boundaries, frontiers divide entities and if those entities don't like each other or are afraid of external influences, they tend to involve all this negative paraphernalia. It doesn't have to be like that, of course. Some countries are mature enough to value their neighbours, including their historic enemies. Crossing borders in those situations is softened, no longer an ordeal but a smooth passage between friends who don't seek to assert superiority but respect each other.

Where there are acknowledged 'Borderlands' they can form part of this pattern: areas of transition, the merging of cultures, perhaps developing cultures of their own, neither quite the same as either of the adjoining territories. Of course, when a borderland is disputed and there's no neatly defined frontier, or powerful rivals seek to expand their zone of control, it may become a Debatable Land, subject to lawless aggression. Even then there may be a shared sense of identity among those inhabiting borderlands, both sides of any line or hatching on the page. That's often not appreciated by those living in the divergent 'heartlands' further from the theoretical border. The denizens of the Scottish Borders over many centuries could tell us something about that. Those they raided across the border were sometimes kith and kin. Interestingly, for centuries these doughty borderers accepted that disputes could be arbitrated by wardens from both sides, meeting locally. That arrangement was more acceptable than interventions from Edinburgh or

London.

It's when borders represent divisions between cultures, races or religions that it can get really problematic, potentially fraught and bloody. Then the very idea of borderlands allowing a gentle transit from one jurisdiction to another becomes anathema to one or both adjoining countries. Sometimes borderlands need to become buffer zones, 'no-man's lands', between antagonistic regimes, separating acquisitive or threatening neighbours, protecting minorities, perhaps patrolled by peace-keeping forces.

Borderlands with a sense of their own identity are intriguing anomalies. Frequently they have been the prize in historic tugs of war: Alsace-Lorraine, Schleswig-Holstein, those Scottish Borders again. Whole countries have been or are essentially borderlands between different historic entities, replicating traditional preconceptions and animosities. The Hapsburg Empire has been gone for a century but animosities and stereotypes fostered within it persist. The effects can be long-lasting. Over the centuries we can trace influences deriving from the break-up of the Carolingian Empire and its division into three following Charlemagne's death. The 'Middle Kingdom' foreshadowed frequently shifting borders between the emergent kingdom of France and the 'Holy Roman Empire of the German People'. Switzerland succeeded in securing its liberty and melded together its citizens speaking different languages and with different affinities. Belgium, much later, was created to do the same; after two centuries, it's probably early days to judge the outcome.

Borders can be both matters of convenience and perception. Where there is a durable tradition of localised administration, even after all the 19th century uprisings to unify divided countries, people in the 21st century may still relate more strongly to their 'länder', regions or provinces than to the unified nation. Affinities are nuanced and subjective matters, but sophisticated citizens can cope with the concept of different layers for different purposes, including groupings of nations. That's true in Western Europe where, by and large, national boundaries are nowadays mostly accepted as a fait accompli. In fact this is very recent and there are still noteworthy exceptions where borders have meaningful and potentially overwhelming significance: we all know about the island of Ireland, Scotland, Catalonia. They deserve a separate lecture.

Administrative divisions are the subject of contention at all levels. Internal boundaries between local authorities in Great Britain are supposed to reconcile, as best they can, provision for effective local government while having regard to arithmetical equality of representation. That's complicated enough but there's a third criterion, the need to reflect the identities of local communities, and that makes the issue much more complex. On the map a railway line might appear to make a good ward boundary but a level-crossing on the edge of a local shopping area can mean there's constant coming and going between recognised 'neighbours'. Elsewhere, the inhabitants of two adjacent and apparently similar villages may resist being in the same ward and the only explanation given is that they'd fought on opposite sides in the 17th century. Folk memory, perceived differences, an unwillingness to change: sometimes physical borders reflect mental borders as much as physical ones.

It's all rather 'borderline', isn't it? That's another weasel-word, used in many contexts: borderline exam result, borderline symptoms, borderline sanity … 'Borderline' implies ambiguity, ambivalence, equivocation. It's not hard and fast, but marginal and uncertain. It evokes borderlands rather than borders. Borderlands and borderline situations are necessary concepts to describe the messy blurring of lines which human life entails. The distinction between communities is not necessarily determined by the existence of the river between them, even when, historically, they were only linked by ferry. That may be inconvenient for administrative purposes but it's nothing like so perplexing to conventional thinkers as the growing comprehension of the borderlands of individual identity.

We all live in personal borderlands, both physical and non-physical. Few communities are clear-cut, particularly in urban areas, and our individual characteristics are best defined as on a spectrum rather than in prescribed compartments relating, for example, to gender, sexual orientation and natural propensities. Complexity is challenging and many look for simplicity. Authoritarians, populists, the rigorously narrow-minded – all look for uniformity, in their own image, denying the borderlands we inhabit in our bodies, minds and souls. These are all considerations we need to approach with open minds.

Oh, it's all so academic! Worthy, well-meaning, but abstract, hypothetical, speculative. I relished theorising but how little I knew. I never referred to the consequences of civil wars. I'll need to rewrite all my lectures, if I ever have the chance. In this beautiful, lofty landscape, I can rehearse all the concepts, weigh up all the merits and demerits of constitutional, administrative, and bureaucratic arguments but on this border reality is the bullet in the head I may receive when I leave my rocky hiding place. The borderland I seek is one of sanctuary, safety, freedom.

It's getting dull already with this overcast sky. It's time for me to creep downhill, step by step, metre by metre. There's no need to hold my breath. No one can hear me. But instinct tells me to muffle the smallest sound. Is that a legacy from hunter-gatherer ancestors? Enough. No more notional analysis. Focus on the terrain and the descent. Concentrate!

*****

Oh, merciful denizens of heaven, if you exist, praise and thanks! Somehow my luck has held, despite the moon coming clear of the clouds. I've reached the lower part of the ravine and I'm completely shielded from above. The rocks at the edge of the water are coming into view. I'll be able to lower myself from one of them and launch out into the river. It's as I hoped. Better – I didn't realise how well those spindly trees on the cliff would screen me. I'll stop for a minute and calm myself. My heart's thumping. It's peaceful here, re-assuring, only the rushing water to soothe my spirits.

I can just make out the far bank of the river. That glow in the distance must be the reception post. My guiding light. The sacred flame on the altar where I'll prostrate myself – metaphorically speaking. Lead kindly light: that's a Christian hymn, I believe. Right-ho, I'll follow its lead. Onward.

Aargh! What's that? Something lying on the rock. A body straddling it, face-down. Surely a dead body? It must have been swept downstream, washed up, marooned there. I have to ignore it. There's nothing I can do. Besides, it might be booby-trapped, put there to destroy anyone who succeeded in getting here without being seen by the guards. I mustn't be distracted. I must go on.

The rock beside the one that's occupied will suit me best. There's an easy drop into the water from that ledge at its side and the surface isn't too jagged. I'll heave myself on top, then step down to the ledge.

Poor fellow. I think it's a man though it's difficult to tell: a large well-built man. I can see there's a wound on his head. It looks quite fresh. Perhaps he was swimming and they shot him. Perhaps he clambered onto the rock hoping he wasn't too badly hurt – or simply to die. I must suppress these useless thoughts.

His family won't know what's happened to him. Probably they'll never hear.

He might have papers in a waterproof wallet, like I have. They'd show who he was, so his death could be notified and recorded – part of the indictment to be tabled one day, another crime to be laid at the door of those monsters who took power. Stop it! Forget the idea! Don't touch him.

No! No! Your eyes are deceiving you. It must be the breeze. Nothing more. His mouth didn't twitch. It isn't possible. Leave him. Go! Get back from him.

No! It is. No! There can't be. A faint murmur. A human murmur. I'll just lean a little closer. To satisfy myself; so I can go on without qualms.

I can see more clearly now. His clothes are ripped. I think there's a wound in his chest as well. There's congealed blood. I can't see any wires but they think up sophisticated traps. I have to leave him. As soon as that cloud covers the moon, I'll slip into the water.

It's true! Oh, dear God, there's a faint breath, a gurgling noise. He's not dead, but he must be dying. There's no way I could move him or get him across the river. There's nothing I can do.

What a lonely, horrible death: after all that must have happened to him. No hint of solace, no human comfort.

If I stroked his hand gently, would he sense my presence? Would it help him?

Don't be a fool. Never mind booby-traps, the longer you delay here the more chance of being discovered. Now, the moon is disappearing. Now. Go.

His fingers are spread out on the surface of the rock, broad, practical fingers, useless fingers. He is alone, of no account, abandoned by the world.

How can I ignore him? How can I deny my own humanity? I would resemble the monsters who caused his death. But I would feel shame.

May my touch bring him a wisp of comfort. May he know someone was with him in the ultimate borderland of his life.

Now.

DIE GRENZE

Recollections of a few days in the German Democratic Republic.

By Michael Hutchinson

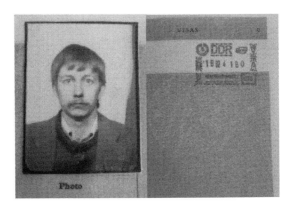

Somewhere ahead, in the teeming darkness of the north German night, a few lights sparkled. We were nearing the border with the Democratic Republic. Soon, we would be behind the Iron Curtain. Renate removed one hand from the steering wheel and dug inside her waistcoat pocket.

'Where do you think we should hide this?' She showed me a small object wrapped in aluminium foil. Cannabis resin.

The border lights grew brighter. As the fence and its watchtowers came into view I tried desperately to think of places the border guards wouldn't think of searching.

'Could we hide it inside the steering wheel?

Renate appeared to consider this option for a moment. Then she pushed the cannabis back inside her pocket. This was how it was going to be.

It was 1982 and I was staying with friends in West Germany. Germany fascinated me. I was particularly keen on the work of the Expressionists, artists like Max Beckmann and Ernst Ludwig Kirchner and there were some excellent galleries in West Germany with collections of their work. I also considered myself a Marxist. I'd read Das Kapital, but understood little of it, and was living in Sheffield, the capital of the so-called Socialist Republic of South Yorkshire. And I'd just visited Friedrich Engel's house in Wüppertal. But I wanted something more. I wanted to go to East Germany. I wanted to go to Berlin.

No sooner had I floated this idea than the boyfriend of my good friend, Ulrike, said that he had a friend who also wanted to visit Berlin. This was how I met Renate Müller. My German friends were generous and responsible people. For example, they'd wait at pedestrian crossings until the lights changed, even if there was no traffic. 'It sets an example to children,' was their explanation, conveyed in an 'isn't it obvious' manner. Renate was different. She told me she was a Zen-Buddhist and a drummer - I never learned much more than that. Her hair was coloured red with some powdery material that managed to get everywhere. It reminded me of powder paint, a medium I've detested ever since using it at school. But Renate was unlike my German friends in other crucial ways, as I was soon to discover.

We passed through the East German border without problem and I began to relax, although relax might have been overstating it. It was February and the cold was more intense than anything I'd ever experienced. To make matters worse, the heating in Renate's old Renault 4 barely worked at all: I noticed that she'd stuffed old tights and socks around the dashboard, presumably in an attempt to keep draughts out. I was wearing a proletariat-chic outfit - donkey jacket, jeans, Doc Martin's - which, more or less, dealt with the cold back in Britain. But not here.

The poorly-lit dual carriageway which linked the Bundesrepublik with West Berlin was almost devoid of traffic. After some time, Renate asked me to drive. It appeared to be a matter of indifference to her that I didn't have a driving license, or that her insurance, if she had any, which I should have queried, wouldn't cover me. Fortunately, my spell behind the wheel didn't last long as I couldn't work the dashboard-mounted gear change and I was soon back in the passenger seat.

Some miles inside East Germany, we spotted a motorway café and, being frozen by this time, pulled into a car park. The café was at the opposite side of the motorway and accessed via an underpass, unlit, and some distance away. After we'd warmed up with something from the limited menu (brown material that may once have possessed legs, potatoes and, inevitably, cabbage) we returned to the car. There was no traffic whatsoever now, and the cold had deepened. Renate suggested a short cut directly across the motorway. So that was what we did. As we approached the car park, I noticed a car parked alongside Renate's Renault. It was green and white and had Polizei written along its side. I was numbed by the cold but more so by the fear that they would search Renate and find the cannabis. How many years for jay-walking across the motorway? How long for possession? My German wasn't very good so I left Renate to talk to the police while I stood and froze nearby. After a lengthy discussion, the police simply issued us with an on-the-spot-fine of ten East German marks. It was nothing. About £2.50 in sterling. Hugely relieved, I paid and was handed a receipt which I pushed into a pocket - I'd keep that as a souvenir. We'd got away with it.

Once in West Berlin Renate drove to the old UFA film studios, the UfaFabrik, now a performing arts centre, but at that time a squat. She knew someone who worked, or lived there - I never understood which - and, so she explained, we'd be able to stay a few nights. Eventually, and more by luck than navigation, we found the building. Renate's friend wasn't there and the person behind the barely opened door was reluctant to let us in. I'd had enough by this time and suggested finding a hotel but Renate wasn't ready to give in. She entered into lengthy negotiations as I stood shivering, yet again, nearby. But her persistence worked, and we were let in. The sleeping accommodation consisted of a huge communal bunk bed. I can't recall how many of us were sharing it although there was at least one other person besides Renate and myself on the top. There were also other occupants, as I was to discover later. However, I was so cold and tired by this stage that I would have crawled into any available space.

Next morning, and after breakfast, my mood had improved. We picked up a companion, an Iranian street musician, who played the mandolin extremely well. I wanted to go into East Berlin; I'd heard that it was possible to buy excellent art books at low prices and hoped to find some. The three of us travelled in using the underground, the U-Bahn. At the border crossing below Friedrichstraße, we had to buy 24-hour visas and change enough of our West German marks for East German ones: this was a one-way transaction as we wouldn't be able to cash in any unused money on the way back out, nor take out any unspent East German marks. That was definitely verboten. However, it all seemed to be going well enough until I was taken into a small room and searched. I had nothing unusual or suspicious on me except for one thing. I still had the receipt for the motorway fine. This interested the border guards for quite some time. I attempted to make light of it, but wasn't very convincing. But eventually I was released and rejoined the others.

We spent our first day in East Berlin wandering around in a rather aimless fashion. It was very quiet compared to the western half of the city. Somewhere near the Brandenburg Gate, Renate, ignoring the red do-not-cross signal, walked into the Unter-den-Linden. There was no traffic and she wasn't taking any risks. But she hadn't seen a nearby policeman. He called her over and yet another discussion ensued. I decided to leave her to it this time and walked away. Renate survived this second encounter with the law, receiving nothing other than a warning.

The following day, Renate suggested going back into the East, but not by the U-Bahn. This time she would drive. We drove to the border crossing at Friedrichstraße, also known by its US name, Checkpoint Charlie. Here things quickly became confusing and very alarming. The East German side looked exactly like a scene from a film adaptation of a John Le-Carré novel: steel fences with gates; watchtowers; border guards in long grey coats topped off by fur hats; guns. I was brusquely ordered out of the car. A couple of guards barked instructions at Renate and she drove away, leaving me in a narrow strip of land separating East and West Berlin. I was summoned forward so went on. First through one gate that was immediately locked behind me. Then through the next and finally into a single-storey building at the side of the street. Here I joined a short queue of people purchasing visas. The man in front of me had two carrier bags of shopping, mostly vegetables from what I could see. A border guard placed these, one at a time, inside a crude x-ray machine - I noticed the word röntgen written on the front, along with a warning symbol. The guard turned a handle and, I assumed, the carrier bags slowly rotated whilst getting a good soaking of x-rays.

When I reached the front of the queue I tried joking with the guard. Perhaps it was my poor German, or because he was having a bad day, but he remained distinctly unfriendly and appeared to view me with suspicion. Nevertheless, I was allowed through and found myself out on the street and wondering what I was going to do now.

After a few minutes had passed, I was surprised to see Renate's Renault turn the corner. They had entered through another crossing without encountering any difficulties. None of us understood what the problem at Friedrichstraße had been but at least we were back together.

The day passed quite pleasantly enough despite the ever present cold. We had tried to get something to eat and drink in one bar, without success, but otherwise everything seemed okay. The bar we'd gone into was filled with men in the now familiar grey coats and fur hats. I didn't know if they were Germans or Russians but I was glad to leave and try somewhere else. What started to nag away at me about our failure to get any food in the bar, and the earlier incident at Checkpoint Charlie, was that we, and especially Renate, a native German speaker, had no idea why we were having problems. My lingering unease and sense of groundlessness was only going to get worse.

We capped off our visit to the East by going to a jazz concert in a very attractive, Baroque-style building. It was past eleven when we turned out, and, as our visas were only valid until midnight, we had to get back into West Berlin very soon. Renate drove to the closest border crossing. We were turned away, again without any explanation. Midnight was approaching as Renate drove alongside the wall towards the next exit. The same thing happened. We were turned away. No explanation yet again. The sense of dread I'd felt on the motorway began to resurface. Then, Renate had a thought. Perhaps we had to return through the crossings we'd entered by? We were nearly out of time now and this seemed our last chance. Renate dropped me off on Friedrichstraße and sped away. My visa was due to expire in just twenty minutes. There wasn't a soul around as I went through one steel gate, which locked solidly behind me, then waited for the next to click open. Time appeared to slow to a crawl with each second reluctant to accede to the next. But finally, I was through the final gate and walking back across that strip of no-man's-land. I wanted to run, or at least quicken my pace, but was painfully conscious of being watched. I'd also seen too many spy films to not know that you never, ever run. Heart in my mouth, I reached the small Allied border post set in the centre of the road. I offered my passport to the man inside who simply smiled and waved me though. I was safe. The whole experience, and particularly this friendly smile, caused some havoc with my left-wing sympathies. A little while later, Renate and our Iranian friend drove up. We'd all made it back.

The next morning, Renate and I left the UfaFabrik and headed back towards West Germany, but not before she explained who the other occupants of the communal bunk were. 'Viele kleiner Tiere,' she said, making a little jumping movement with one hand. 'Many little animals.' That explained the small itchy red spots I'd discovered around my ankles. Just before we reached the crossing point from West Berlin back into East Germany, Renate had one last revelation. From inside her waistcoat pocket she produced the remainder of the dope. It was obvious, even to Renate, that we couldn't risk crossing the border with this a second time. She could simply have tossed it out of the car window but seemed very reluctant to do this. The lingering traces of a Lutheran upbringing, I wondered? I did the gallant thing and smoked it all in the car before we left West Berlin.

The remainder of the journey was uneventful and has largely lapsed from my memory, something probably not helped by the cannabis. I stayed with Renate in Cologne for a further night and, on the following day, caught a train taking me to a channel port. Once back in Sheffield, life felt safe but boring. Although I'd never been someone who craved excitement, for a while I really missed it. I wanted to return to Germany, get a job, get a studio. But time passed, and the addiction to what had probably been a surfeit of adrenaline subsided. I quietly abandoned the idea.

I never had any contact with Renate Müller again but returned to Berlin after the Wall fell and the two parts of Germany were reunified. I didn't recognise Friedrichstraße at all without its steel fences and watchtowers. Men dressed as East German border guards are still there, but now only pose for tourists to have their photographs taken with.

Somewhere in the intervening years, I lost my souvenir - the fine Renate and I received for jay-walking across the motorway. But I do have two small pieces of the original Berlin Wall, a gift from my son when he visited Berlin. The accompanying certificate states that they are genuine and a piece of German history. And I've thought about how many millions of such souvenirs must have been sold, and for how much in total. Perhaps it's time to read Das Kapital again?

ONE DAY ON ST CUTHBERT'S WAY

By Anita John

Walk's eve, a blackbird serenades

from a chimney pot;

collar doves coo-coo us awake

walk's dawn.

In a green field, two roe deer leap

through grass,

extended legs suspended mid-air,

pointing to the path's curl

hillward, out of sight.

Skylarks throw sonic notes

under clouded sky,

clouded blaeberries

underfoot

all the way to the top.

Wide Open Hill.

Barbed-wire fence

wind-singing.

We sing too

***

Wind and well-worn signs

leading downwards

past short-grassed moor,

deciduous and conifers,

the meadows of Kale Water.

Grey wagtail, dipper, the brilliance

of yellowhammer in flight.

A hawthorn hedge

with blackbird serenading,

two roe deer grazing a fallow field

with weeds and wild flowers.

Then tarmac, tarmac underfoot…

Each pilgrimage

small miracle and penance.

FOREST BATHING

By Elizabeth Kelly

I step from solid light

into droplets that wash

over my skin,

settle in a sheen

across my face.

Wild garlic's scent

sheds into the air,

as rich as colour against

decaying leaves.

I touch silver bark,

it flakes like ancient paper,

I attach my words,

watch them float to the earth,

mingle with the soil.

I let them go.

THE MAGIC OF READING

By Toni Parks

Treasure Island left Logan's hand at the exact split second the library's clock began its announcement of two pm. By the time the book reached its destination the timepiece was in the process of chiming the last of its two dongs. Miss Constance, librarian, situated in Young Readers' corner, slowly raised her candyfloss, grey-haired head revealing a pair of spectacles camouflaged within. With a jerky nod she transferred them onto her nose, all the better to access the situation. First, she looked at the discarded book's position on the linoleum floor and then, rewound the trajectory of the throw in her mind to ascertain the culprit. Another nod of the candyfloss, less severe this time, accompanied by a 'Humph' led her to conclude that Logan Andrews was the one in need of a good talking to.

Stepping down from her counter stool she walked slowly, fairy-step like, towards a red-faced boy of maybe nine wearing a face like thunder.

'Now, young man, to what do we owe this act of violence?' she asked, in a level voice.

'Violence? I've not touched anyone, Miss.'

'Oh, but you have, albeit not another person, you have been aggressive towards an object.' Miss Constance walked as she spoke, and stooping down retrieved the book from the floor. 'You've taken out your anger on one of the town's possessions.' Turning the book she revealed its title. 'An important work too.'

'Not important to me, is it. I'd rather be out with my mates playing football, not here with my sister, while Mum shops.'

'Ah, the library's doing a spot of babysitting, is it. And where is your sister, might I ask?'

'She's in the grown-up bit. Searching for something, she said. To do with her school work, she said.'

'Researching is the word you're looking for. Good for her. You ought to take a leaf out of her book. Don't books interest you the same? Don't you enjoy reading?' she asked, slowly ushering him to the alcove predominantly containing books for boys.

'No, 'cause I can't read properly. My eyes get tired, my mind starts wandering and I get bored. And, anyway, I can never remember what I've read. My Mum says I've probably got visible stress or that I'm ...' here Logan paused, raised his eyes to the heavens, and then continued '... it's a word that rhymes with Scalextric'.

'Mmm, I think she'll have said visual stress and the word you're looking for is dyslexic,' chuckled Miss Constance. 'Do you find the words move when you read or do some of the letters appear in the wrong order or the wrong way round?'

'Yes, and at other times I see white gaps running down pages between the words, which seem to stand out more than the words themselves.'

'Perhaps, you need a colour overlay to make the words easier on the eye, or you may even need to wear reading-glasses, as I do.'

Logan stared at the old lady's face in horror.

Miss Constance understood the meaning of his shocked expression. 'No, no, they wouldn't have to look like mine; you'd get to choose a pair that suits your face. Well, maybe not the angry face, hey.'

'So, why do you enjoy reading so much?' asked Logan. 'I mean you must do to sit with all these books everyday.'

'Oh, I do, I do enjoy it. I've always found it so magical. Reading takes me away to mystical lands where princes and princesses live, to Africa where all the animals roam, to sailing on the seven seas – but enough about me. Let's sit until your sister comes for you and I'll give you some tips on how to read without your mind wandering or getting bored.

'First of all, you must clear out what's already in your head – a bit like tidying your room. Everything has to go back to where it belongs, either the wardrobe, a drawer or the wash basket, even those plates, bowls and glasses need taking back to the kitchen.'

Logan grinned at the joke, even though he was fogged as to how she knew his room.

'Now we've freed up space for your concentration to take over. You do know what that is, don't you?'

'When you think deeply about one specific thing?' he suggested, tentatively.

'Yes, Logan, and as well as concentration you also need imagination. Know what that is too?'

Here, Logan grinned and nodded, both at the same time. 'Yes, that's pretending, isn't it?'

'Very good. We're getting somewhere. If you'd have carried on with Treasure Island instead of ...' Miss Constance thought better of continuing on that tack and said instead, '... you might have imagined you were Jim Hawkins, the cabin boy amongst all those pirates. But not to worry, we just need to find a book that will stimulate both your concentration and imagination and create a magical world for you.'

Miss Constance sitting on one of the low chairs, hands on knees, studied the bookshelf opposite. Suddenly, she jumped up, reached out and tugged at a faded spine tucked away between many more colourful and bolder ones.

'This is the one for you. I've not seen it around for years as it's usually out on loan, but I remember it well.'

She turned to face Logan and presented its front cover - a montage of illustrations, featuring men riding horses and waving swords in the air, dirty-faced boys no older than Jim Hawkins himself, dressed in an array of colourful and sombre misshapen clothes, armed only with long pointed sticks and short daggers. At its centre was a photo of a submarine positioned so as to give the illusion it was protruding forwards, directly out of the cover itself, close by a head and shoulders photograph of a serious looking man in uniform.

The title curved from left to right above their heads like an umbrella. Logan read it out loud, 'Borderlands,' and smiled for the first time that morning. Underneath in smaller text, he continued, 'And some famous and not-so-famous characters who lived there'.

Miss Constance turned to the page showing the list of borrowers and enthusiastically remarked, 'Logan, this is definitely the one for you. It was only returned yesterday after being out on loan continuously for two years! That must be a record for this library. I suggest that you book this out and take it home. Read it when you're tucked up in bed. That way you can tidy out your brain and be in a receptive frame of mind to experience an adventure or two with perhaps a few mishaps as well.'

Logan didn't feel quite as enthusiastic about the book as Miss Constance, particularly as when she'd flicked through the pages, there weren't many pictures to be seen, but her energy rubbed off on him and his imagination was beginning to fire up.

When Logan's sister returned she was pleasantly surprised to find him patiently waiting at the exit and clutching a library book under his arm. Once home, Borderlands went one way and Logan another, not to be reunited until a timely reminder by Mrs Andrews that bedtime was fast approaching and asking if he was looking forward to delving into his own heritage and history.

Logan, in two minds, eventually took the book and then the stairs. He thought about Miss Constance's joy and enthusiasm for reading as opposed to his own indifference. But at least he could give it a go for nothing and maybe he might just surprise himself with the result.

Snug in his bed he held the book and traced a finger over the collage of images depicted on the cover. His brain took in their strange dress, aggressive yet boyish looks, deadly weapons and muscular horses, while at the same time packing away the everyday humdrum thoughts usually nestling there. Being new to reading for pleasure, a phrase his mother had often bombarded him with, he opened it gingerly and turned to the well-thumbed title page in search of adventure.

The Battle of Hornshole appeared before him. 'Hornshole,' what did that mean? Already a question and he'd not got past the title. Read on and all will be revealed, Logan, said the book. And so he did. He noticed that the words stayed fixed in position with no movement or gaps appearing as had often happened before leaving him frustrated and confused. None of the letters had reversed themselves and the 'ds' and 'bs' were on their best behaviour, he understood both with ease. And where were the white rivers flowing down the page? Not there came the answer. Perhaps, it was the easy-to-read typeface, or the off-white colour of the paper on which the story had been printed. Or perhaps, there was a magical quality to the book as alluded to by Miss Constance. Why would it be loaned out so often if that were not the case, questioned Logan?

Logan read. The story gripped his imagination like nothing ever before. Subconsciously the words began to merge into each other until only a straight black line remained. But this didn't bother Logan, as he knew instinctively what was expected of him. In his mind's eye he took hold of the black line and raised it up, in cowboy lasso fashion, and threw it around one of the characters depicted on the front cover.

Instantly, it was dead of night and Logan, holding only his stout wooden club tightly to his chest, crashed through the undergrowth by the side of the river Teviot. A severe loss of Hawick men at the battle of Flodden in 1513, had left the town extremely undermanned and vulnerable to attack, so boys' transition to men had come quickly indeed. And now, only a year later, he and his friends recognised the responsibility in safeguarding their neighbours from perceived English raiders camped out at Hornshole.

Having run nigh on two miles eastwards with only a pale sickle of a moon above illuminating his way and a low lying mist hanging over the river to his left, Logan thanked the Lord as the command "Halt!" was whispered amongst his comrades. Sweat and fear permeated the air blending with the already sour stench of acute body odour and the pungent smell of unwashed clothing. And as his beating heart slowed he too heard, above the gurgles and rocks tumbling in the fast flowing river, the sound of laughter and merriment some distance in front. Their leader, so chosen as being the eldest, ordered two subordinates to scout ahead, then mingled among his fellow warriors and offered encouragement and optimism for the task in hand. He surmised that the element of surprise and lack of light, God's will permitting, would be to their advantage. He explained the lie of the land; where he anticipated the enemy to be camped; where the horses and other livestock would most likely be tethered, close by the deep pool so named Hornshole, and even anticipated where the sentries would be posted.

The scouts returned. Logan wished the wait longer but knew the time for wavering was long gone and the onslaught of his first battle was imminent. At least darkness hid the fright etched on his timid face but it would not steal away his worrying thoughts - they still lingered.

The leader summoned a dozen youths to represent the phalanx of the assault with everyone else following in close formation behind. No sooner planned than executed. The young Hawick warriors stormed the English camp with the scream of murder renting the air as pikes, swords, daggers, clubs and farm implements waved aloft in search of heads to cleave and bust.

Logan's wooden club met bone on more than one occasion. He swung without fear or favour, a red mist descending on his eyes egging him on to avenge the tragic loss of his forebears at Flodden. Once the English had been routed he was found clutching their pennant, the previous holder prostrate at his feet.

In Hawick's Main Street, the Battle of Hornshole is immortalised by a bronze statue depicting a youth riding horseback with the captured trophy pennant raised skywards. The unnamed rider represents the fighting spirit of the Borders just as the First World War's unknown warrior is in honour to the sacrificed lives of unknown soldiers everywhere.

Logan's mother marched into her son's bedroom, her face mirroring the thunder outside that should have awoken the most ardent sleepyhead. Instead, a heaped pile of duvet on the floor and an upended book but no Logan greeted her. She called out his name for the second time that morning only now with a hint of inquisitiveness. As if by magic, the duvet moved in response and a mass of unruly hair emerged, followed by the rest of Logan's yawning head.

'Is it time for school, already?' he mumbled through the longest yawn in Christendom, or so it seemed.

'It certainly is, lovey, and we'll all be late if you don't shake yourself.

What made you fall out of bed? You've not done that in a long time' said his mother, sweeping the duvet up off the floor and relaying it across his bed.

'Mmm, must have been an energetic dream with lots of running and fighting. But at least I appear to be in one piece.'

'I'll give you one piece. In the bathroom with you,' admonished his mum. Which reminded him. He raised his arms, sniffed underneath and smelled only the usual Logan odour. All was well. 'And I want to see you sitting at the kitchen table in five minutes, in uniform! Your toast will be waiting,' she continued.

The toast didn't wait long before being demolished, testament to Logan's appetite. Had time permitted another slice or two would have been appreciated but no such luck as it was of the essence with everyone now running late, somewhat incongruous to the rest of Logan's day, which hung heavy like the drag of a hundredweight anchor holding back the hours.

But bedtime arrived eventually, or near enough anyway, and Logan's yawns preceded his eager steps up to bed, to which surprisingly no one raised a quizzical eyebrow.

Duvet tucked under his chin he feasted on the Borderlands' topics like a ravenous diner feverishly scanning a menu. Spoilt for choice between - the adventures of Anthony Blair Fasson, born in the village of Lanton near Jedburgh, the recipient of a posthumous George Cross for retrieving an Enigma Machine from a scuttled German submarine during the Second World War – and the Selkirk weaver named Fletcher, sole returnee from Flodden, struck dumb by the sight of his comrades' deaths at that disastrous battle.

But whichever story he hitched his black line to he knew it would be the right one, in the same way he knew why this particular book spent far longer being loaned out than it did gathering dust on a library bookshelf.

DOORS

By Jane Pearn

I don't turn round at the knock at the door in case there's no-one there. It's ajar anyway: there's no need to shut it because there's no-one to disturb me. It's been three months and three days since I last needed to close it. May 23rd. Jen always knocked the same way. Short-long-short-long. Like our own private Morse code, it was all in the rhythm. We used to say it meant *Is it okay? Can I come in?*

I liked to hear her moving around in her studio above my head, I would know by the creak of a certain floorboard if she'd stepped back from the easel to take a longer view. Towards completion of a picture, those steps backwards and forwards would become more frequent as she made tiny adjustments - a hint of green, a slightly deeper shadow.

In spring and summer, the background sounds would include the stop-start of the lawnmower, or if my window was open, the tiny snick of secateurs. Jen looked after the garden mostly. She has an eye for shape and colour and form and balance. A good cook too. Before Jen, I'd always lived alone and I've never been very domesticated. She found my laisser-faire attitude exasperating at times. Later she called it practised incompetence.

We met at a gallery where Jen was exhibiting. She was no beauty but her long, narrow, intelligent, amused face immediately attracted me. She was as thin and straight as one of her pencils. Soon after we met, she told me that at art college she'd been known as Jen the Pen, partly because of her spare figure, but also for the calligraphic flourish she used to sign her work. She loved my curves and what she called my sumptuousness. I posed for her often, and the pictures sold well. The poorly insulated attic required several heaters if she needed me nude.

Later, if we'd celebrated a sale with a couple of bottles of good red, she'd call me Susie the Floozie. The next morning, I was never sure if I should have minded or not. But I let it go. To be with her was as if a door had suddenly swung open to let in light and life and possibilities when I had thought it was locked for ever, and that I would never know what lay on the other side. We were Ying and Yang, cup and saucer, hand and glove. In those early, heady days we argued delightedly about who was the hand and who the glove.

Her children accepted our relationship without fuss. Her once-husband Don had left his family to live with the sculptor Camilla Lockhart, when the kids were teenagers. Now they were both grown-up and didn't feel they owed him much loyalty. Max had recently married Oliver, and Jetta was currently single. I gathered Jen had had a few brief flings, with women and

48

men both, so they were unsurprised, and even seemed genuinely pleased that she'd settled down with me. The age difference didn't bother them. Although I'm ten years younger than Jen, I'm still older than them, and that probably helped. I never met Don in person but of course I'd read his work and seen him on telly, heavy-jowled, unshaven, wild hair, every inch the creative genius that people described. Sometimes I felt the image was consciously cultivated. The novels are wonderful though. Jen didn't talk much about him, but I gathered he wasn't easy to live with, expecting her to cope with most of the day-to-day routine of marriage and children and house.

We found our own house, tucked at the end of a town terrace, tall and thin. The attic was Jen's studio and below her my writing den, once the spare room. It meant guests had to sleep on the sofa-bed downstairs but that was a rarity. We were too wrapped up in our work and each other to want many visitors.

When I was writing, I needed my door shut even if it was only Jen in the house. It was my way of saying I'm in mid-thought, don't break it. We rarely interrupted each other. My signal to Jen was to gently scratch with my nail on her door. Scratch-scraatch-scratch-scraatch. It might be open in any case. She sometimes needed to step back onto the landing to take an even longer view. I scratched because I said, If you can't be disturbed, you can just pretend it's a mouse behind the skirting and take no notice. And I'll creep away again, just like a mouse.

I miss seeing her ramrod straight back, the way she was so absorbed in what she was doing that she existed in an invisible column of concentration. Sometimes I would watch her before scratching on the door. Maybe she knew I was there all along, but she would turn unhurriedly at the sound with a wide slow smile.

I don't quite know how it happened. One day I said, almost in passing, that I wasn't quite so keen on her latest work. It seemed such a little thing, but perhaps there was a current under the surface we'd both been ignoring. A slight tetchiness, an irritability with each other's small foibles that had once seemed so endearing. Perhaps these moments were like the bits of loose gravel they say bounce down the mountain before an eruption, an early indicator of subterranean forces. And eruption it certainly was. Why did I insist on selfishly shutting myself away for hours when there was work to be done, and why was it that Jen had to take responsibility for the garden? She tore, unnecessarily brutally I thought, into my latest collection. Called it self-indulgent, wondered why my publisher hadn't edited more ruthlessly, and generally gave me to understand that I wasn't as good as I thought I was. Worse still, she said, 'You're just like Don.'

It turned out that Don had been in contact over the past few weeks, wanting to get back together with her. Camilla had ditched him and he'd been unwell and felt vulnerable. But I think that was just an excuse Jen made, to make her feel better about leaving me. From what I'd gleaned, he hadn't changed his spots and there wasn't going to be a happy reunion. And if I was like him, she wasn't going to exchange one Don for another.

Both shocked by the suddenness of the split, we agreed to give each other a complete break, and after the initial flurry of practical arrangements, not be in contact. We tried to be cordial, but those last few days, I couldn't look her in the face. Jen found herself a small studio flat to rent 300 miles away from me and 250 miles closer to Don. She packed her bags and her paints and her canvases, and left. I stayed here, trying to ignore the For Sale sign in the street. It might as well have said It's over. She's gone.

I'm sad and I'm angry. Angry with Jen, but also angry with myself for not noticing that our relationship was changing, was going wrong, for not trying harder to put it right. But I'm glad it happened, I'm glad Jen happened. It has been the best three years of my life, and the most productive. I think of her often and wonder what, who, she's painting now.

To be honest I'm not in this room so often nowadays, and not writing as much, though I still have my lecturing commitments. I hadn't realised how much work the garden needed in these summer months, or what Jen had done to keep the house, so much more demanding than my old flat, running smoothly. And of course, I have to keep it clean and tidy for prospective buyers.

But a local festival has commissioned a poem and I'm glad of the incentive. So today, on a warm, drowsy late-summer morning I am at my desk. Sometimes I imagine the sound of Jen's footsteps overhead, and I know it's wishful thinking, that I'm allowing my brain, or rather my heart, to invent what it wants to hear. But this, the familiar dot-dash-dot-dash of knuckle on wood? This sounds real.

A message pings in at the corner of my screen. Usually I'm quite self-disciplined and I don't let these distract me. But this time, I glance at it. It's Jen.

I can hear a scratching at my door. Is that you?

ON WINDS, CROSSING

By Cate l. Ryan

Sirocco winds catch hold

the folded lines,

ink wet

when inside paper wings

I sent;

the words you've heard,

said times before,

true yet,

rewritten:

A kind of amulet,

link to reach

your elusive continent -

impossible divide?

I, outside,

imagine paper chased

on desert winds,

see small wings

crossing.

SEA CHANGE

By Cate L. Ryan

First light:

the changing sea,

white-flecked

in winds' cold blast,

quickens to

the milky horizon.

I hug this day;

reflections

of snow-pillows

and leaden down.

You,

a whisper away.

Emerging, fragile

traces

of limbs, minds,

new entwined,

finding

we dare to hold.

DUST BLOWING

By Margaret Skea

Dawn is a long time coming. It will be colder today. Ahmed is hunched over the fire and I am hunched at the mouth of my tent. Last night I could not sleep and Ahmed would not. He stayed close, but not too close, wrapped tight in his patched burnous, his body blocking the worst of the growing north wind.

In the last nine hours - is it only nine hours? - each time I looked up he turned to me, his dark eyes barely focused, seeming as if he were about to speak, but did not. Last night, he said kindly, 'David, there is but a single donkey now, and every day the snow is nearer.'

That is all.

I know, I know. The border is at least three days away, the distant guns and bombs never stop, and yes, I know that the first winter snow is a week overdue, that we cannot force our way through if it comes. But Ahmed, dear, stupid, old man, do you really think that makes me feel better?

Around us the camp is stirring, silence separating into small sounds: the rhythmic flapping of canvas, sandals scuffling the hard-packed earth, a baby grizzling, unable to feed. I move towards the fire, where Ahmed coaxes a flame from cigarette-sized curls of smoke, shielding it from the gusting of the wind until it burns steadily, the odour of donkey dung hanging pungent in the air.

Ahmed glances upward as my shadow falls across him, his eyes betraying nothing. He nods and gestures towards the half-empty water-bag. I crouch beside him and tip my head to trickle water into my mouth, swilling it round and round, trying to swell the volume with saliva, to wash the grit from between my teeth, the fur from my tongue. I dare not take much, for last night we collected only what little we could distil from the dew that fell with dusk.

We did not have the heart to dig.

A handful of children drift towards the fire and huddle close, rubbing with raw knuckles at the smoke spiralling into their eyes. They no longer play in the hour before we break camp. When we began this journey I would wake to scuffles and giggles outside my tent, with Nazim, always more forward than the rest, poking a stick through a finger-picked gap in the rough lacing to prod the soles of my feet stretched out beyond the thin blankets. I used to lie, pretending sleep, for just long enough, then rise with a roar, scattering the children beyond arm's length, their laughter high and infectious.

There is no laughter now. No Nazim.

Between the tents, in the bare space that counts for community here, the women, surrounded by opened bundles, sort the remains of their lives

53

into two unequal piles. The discard pile grows, while what we can carry with us shrivels to less than necessity. With only one donkey remaining, there is nothing else to do.

Once, swelled with responsibility, I led donkeys roped together in strings of twenty or more - heaped with blankets, medicines and foods - aid transferred from the UNICEF lorries halted at Chitral. We crossed by the Shah Saleem pass, driving high into the mountains, playing at 'cat and mouse' with winter and the warlords.

And though both chase us still, this is a very different journey.

Then we travelled northwards, clawing our way along paths no wider than our shoulders, scree slithering beneath our feet, stones scattering into the valley below. Often the leading donkey, shying at hidden bogies, would stop and refuse to budge, so that the others bunched up behind him, nipping haunches, stamping and kicking, their cargo swaying dangerously. Ahmed would scrabble past from the rear, like a mountain goat, alternately cajoling and cursing, pushing while I pulled, beating the donkey while I tempted it with sugar, until, without warning, it would flick its ears and lurch forward, butting me in the stomach, so that I fell sprawling in the dust, while it stepped over me delicately and plodded on.

Ahmed's laughter irritated me then. I would welcome it now.

As I get up the women raise their eyes, but there is no life in them. They do not say so, but I have helped to make it thus. One mother rolling a pillow deftly, one-handed, is with the other gently stroking the cheek of her child, who curls foetus-like, on a blanket by her side, coughing fitfully, his chest jerking. I look away for fear that I will see stirring a new appeal. It would be easier for me if they still wore the burqa, but perhaps I do not deserve ease. Something of them all died with Nazim. Something in me also.

Their eyes drop again to their children, but they do not ask for food, for they know there is none to give.

Behind me, Ahmed has begun to strike the tents. When I join him, we work together silently, releasing the ropes and pulling free the poles, so that the canvases slump to the ground, reminding me of the camels in the souk at Chaghcharan, when caravans still passed through the Ghowr. It is not so very long ago, but the world has changed, as I have. We pack the tents tightly, in stout bundles. I envy Ahmed, who will carry his with ease, belying his greater age, walking with the long, upright stride of the tribesman, the pack steady on his back. For all my practice, I cannot match him, and in that there is danger for us all. But it is necessary that I take my share. When Mahmoud, the last of the young men, melted away to join the resistance fighters in Panjshir province, much of his portion fell to me. I could not find it in my heart to blame him, for there he may find action, or at least talk.

There is little talk between us now, but it does not leave us silence. The sky is etched with the vapour trails of B52s and the sounds of the bombardments grow daily more constant. It is to the east of us now, fluorescent bursts of light shredding the horizon, and I think of Ghazni, of resting between convoys. Of the smell of oil burning in the flickering lamps as dusk swooped upon us. Of sitting cross-legged around the shiisha, the soft sibilant hubble-bubble lulling us as we passed the pipe from hand to hand. It may be that we will sit there again, but I do not think so. Only the babies cry now when the planes go over, the older children do not even raise their heads.

Without Nazim, they too are rudderless.

He was scooping out the sand for a makeshift well, holding the ragged-edged tin in both hands, when the ground erupted under his fingers, catapulting him through the air. It was Ahmed who ran to him, oblivious of other mines, Ahmed who brought him to safe ground. I ran to my tent and scrabbled around in my belongings for the first aid box and something to ease his pain. I gave him morphine, but it was Ahmed, who, when he felt the boy's limbs go limp, removed the metal from his wounds and stitched them as best he could, Ahmed who laid him gently in his tent.

I knew then, I thought then - who could carry him?

At one in the afternoon, with the noise of bombing echoing in the hills to the north and east, I gave Nazim the last of the morphine and watched his face smooth into sleep. When he woke again at four, Ahmed reached out and touched my arm. I looked up at him. We were thinking the same thing - we had to be - the one donkey, the other children, the snow, which any day now would sweep down from the hills and blanket the valleys, in drifts blown fifteen, twenty feet deep by the strong winter winds. I needed him to say something, to understand, to give consent. I had part-trained him - it could have been me who tripped a land-mine, my 'Ahmed, this is how you use a syringe: always expel a little liquid' an unconscious echo of that other trainer, in that other world, when, clumsy-fingered, I shot a stream of water arching into the air. Now, when I lifted the empty syringe and shook my head, pulling the plunger back, he did not meet my eye, only, without a word, twisted the stick in the binding around Nazim's arm as I had shown him, so that the vein in the elbow bloomed. I waited for a moment, head bowed, then, swallowing the saliva rush in my mouth, flicked my finger twice against the vein, eased the needle into position, and pushed.

It was much easier than I expected. It is much less easy now.

Nazim slipped away quietly, his face pale, but free from pain, and we buried him at sunset, wrapped in the bloodstained blanket, in a shallow grave covered in stones scoured from the hillside. On one, larger and flatter than the rest, Ahmed scratched Nazim al-Haq - Shu Jah - 'brave one' and propped it up at the head. As he rose I put out my hand in a clumsy, foreign gesture, and he touched it briefly, whispering 'Shukran', before turning away.

I do not think that I deserve thanks.

In three more days we should make the pass at Zareh Sharan. It may be that they will allow us through - to the border and a measure of hope. Ahmed, his expression carefully blank, moves to the smouldering remains of the fire and begins to rake at it noisily with a stick. The syringe lies in my box, the needle wrapped tightly in cotton-wool. I dare not think that I will use it again. When the fire is dead and the ashes scattered, we shoulder our bundles and move slowly southwards, the women and children straggling after us in a thin line.

Underfoot a pocket of sand shifts and I slip sideways, swallowed ankle-deep. Ahmed reaches out a steadying hand to my elbow, but when I lift my head in thanks his gaze remains fixed on the horizon and he does not turn. And I see that we have each begun another, more difficult journey, but I cannot tell how it will end.

Only one thing is certain.

The dust blows always from the north and it carries away our footprints in the sand.

OUR WINTER WORK ON THE ANIMAL SANCTUARY
Expressed in a modern spirit of the *Carmina Gadelica**

By Barbara Usher

Birther
May we be midwives to your purpose
as we prepare the food stations,
break the ice on white filigree etched water troughs,
carry pails of water across hog wallows
criss-crossed with vegetation
and frost-hardened into mud like chocolate coconut ice.
Our sheep dogs supervise.

Saviour
May we work for you, as co-redeemers, wresting happiness out of pain
so that we may all have a chance to live and hope again.
May our pigs snuffle endearments into the warm straw
as they lie top to tail, nose upturned at their ark door,
may our hens enjoy clearing the polytunnel of greens
and 'passing the harp' noisily through long winter sleeps,
may our sheep enjoy hay as the wind blows hard,
their three generations of families safe on Noah's Arks.

Spirit
You have blown us here, across the Border
may we breathe your creative energy
like a prayer wheel, scattering a gratuitous generosity of blessings,
warming all sentient beings across these fields, this community, this land.

*The Carmina Gadelica is a collection of prayers by 19th and 20th century
Scottish Highlanders and Islanders, orally collected and written down by
Alexander Carmichael. Many of these prayers detail their daily work, asking for
God's protection and blessing on it. Many are in Trinitarian form.

THE EYE OF THE STORM

By Patricia Watts

On the evening of 13th October 1881, many of the fishermen of Eyemouth gathered in The Ship, their local pub, alongside the harbour wall.

Upspoke young Johnny, 'Looks like we'll be able to put to sea in the mornin'. Storm's abated. Seems pretty calm now.'

'Nae, laddy. The storm's just restin'. The glass's droppin'. Never before've we seen it so low. Far too risky,' answered old Jock, wiping the dregs of his pint from his beard, with a gnarled hand. A hand weathered brown from many years of exposure to the elements; a hand calloused from reeling in miles of fishing lines over the years, heavy with resisting fish.

'I agree with you,' piped up Jack Collins. It doesn't look settled to me and I met the Kingfisher this mornin'. He kept telling me the "earthquake's not over yet".'

'Yea, but he's not quite right upstairs now. Should'nae take much notice of him, besides he hasn't got a wife and family to feed,' replied Johnny.

'Ah! But if you go out and the storm takes over, your bairns won't get fed no more,' answered Jack.

The chatter continued; the drinking continued.

'Billy wed that McDougal lassie, Mary, this mornin', early, y'know. The minister wasn't too pleased at having to get up at half past five in this mornin but Billy and his new missus wanted to get off to Edinburgh for the day. He said he'd be back in time to join his crew tomorrow if they put out, so not to worry about a substitute. Hope he's right and gets home. If the storm picks up again travelling might be a problem,' said George.

1

'Mary's a bonny lass, works hard, lives with her parents since she was widowed a couple of years ago. Her husband, James, was blown overboard in the last big storm. His body was never found. T'was a bad job,' answered Jack.

'She already has four bairns and rumour has it that there's another on the way,' went on Jack. 'She's down at the harbour regular, mending nets all day and she's already been up to bait the lines for her father.'

'Aye she's a good lass,' agreed George. 'Hope it works out for them. How about a wee dram to toast their happiness? Drinks all round on me.'

In the Spring of 1881, the small fishing town of Eyemouth experienced the relentless storms that raged down the North East coast of Scotland. Thousands of trees were ripped from their roots and hundreds of homes were flattened. The good catches of the 1870s and 80s that had given the fisher-folk a false sense of security, had dwindled. No one was expecting this and nobody had put anything aside for the bad times. The fisher-folk lived from hand to mouth. The winter haddock catch had shrunk and now the spring catch, everyone was awaiting, was poor and the summer herring season, or the silver darlings as they were called, broke early.

It was not just that the fishermen were affected by the poor fishing but the economy of the whole community that relied on it was brought to a standstill. The live baiters, carters, hawkers, coopers and curing yards all suffered. It was difficult for families to feed and clothe their children, many of whom went hungry. Not only had they little food to sustain them, they often had no more than thin rags of clothes to [2] keep them from the biting winds. The community was made up of large, extended and interconnected families. Two or more of them often lived under one roof. They all relied on one another. Those who were not catching the fish were employed doing other work.

Many of the wives would be up very early to bait the lines with limpets and mussels, as many as 1200 to a line. Each crew member had two lines. The sanitary conditions were poor. The town reeked from the discarded shells of seafood bait tossed into the streets over which hung a thick haze of pungent, choking, smoke from the curing yards.

Eyemouth had suffered from lack of investment into the harbour, due mainly to disputes over the fishing tithes but the residents of the town lived in hope. They had long been promised better times ahead but those times never came. So for a number of reasons at the beginning of October 1881, poverty stricken fishermen were desperate to push out to sea and bring in the catch which would help them put food into the mouths of their children before the next winter. The storm had abated the day before and an eerie calm hung over the town. The Hurkurs loomed large at the harbour head, a menacing grey; hungry looking jaws, ready to snap any vessel that dared enter its reaches. A number of the old sea salts, wearing worried expressions gathered around the weather-glass that had dropped to the lowest point any of them could remember. The women folk, anxious, followed clutching wailing bairns and young children clinging to their skirts. What would the following day bring? Would their men sail? No other fleet up the coast was ready to put to sea so it appeared that the Eyemouth fishermen were preparing to take a great risk. It was mainly driven by the younger members of the crews all anxious to get bread on the table.

So it was on the morning of 14th October 1881, the young women and children had been up early and baited the lines while their menfolk slept off the drink of the night before. At dawn break, the crews, their heavy sea boots slung across their shoulders, and carrying the 'skulls' with ready baited lines, made their way to the boats which were floating, innocently, on the beguiling peaceful waters of the harbour. The sea was calm, ghostly calm. An anaemic sun shone from a cloudless blue, but cold sky. The atmosphere felt hauntingly unusual. Mothers, wives and children gathered on the pier and the beach to wave their men good luck.

The minister made his way back to the manse after an early wedding. He was already weary from burials caused by the storms that had wreaked havoc in the previous months but weddings and burials always took place in the early hours to allow all the crew to be free for fishing.

On his way to join the other five members of his crew was Lenny. He was already running late when who should he bump into but the minister. Now fishermen have many superstitions, one of which is to start the journey again if they should meet either a minister or a woman. Lenny hesitated, normally he would have ignored the superstition but, because of the doubt surrounding their decision to fish today he felt compelled to turn around and restart his journey. He reached his home in double quick time. However, he arrived to find that his mother, herself a widow to the sea, had fallen and was in desperate need of medical attention. He had no alternative but to find the nearest doctor.

'Don't you worry aboot me,' said his mother. 'They'll not think much of you if you're not there to sail with the rest.'

Lenny knew in his heart this would look as though he was trying to avoid the sailing but he could not bring himself to leave his mother.

By this time the first boat, the 'Silver Cloud' pushed out and the other thirty nine followed. Once one boat had put to sea it was a matter of honour for the rest of the fleet to follow. With hardly a breath of wind the sails were of little use so they rowed, with strong arms, in tranquil conditions. Those gathered on the pier to wave them good luck watched full of apprehension as the boats rounded the Hurkurs, defying the warning signs. The ships began to look small and insignificant as they were gradually lost to vision. They would expect to reach the haddock fishing ground, some twelve miles distant, by noon that day. The women folk returned home to their daily tasks.

After about an hour's sailing the sky suddenly turned to a leaden grey, the gentle breeze shifted to a frenzied North Easterly gale. Before the skippers and their crews realised what was happening the sea was in a violent rage, whipped into a boiling cauldron of foam; huge waves broke over the boats, lashing down in tremendous highs and troughs. Sails were torn and poles ripped out. Boats were tossed like toys clean out of the water, their men flying through the air, only to meet a watery death. Some skippers tried to ride the storm and made further out to sea while others tried to sail for home, some of whom reached the Hurkurs only to be dashed onto the rocks in view of their distraught families. Women, old fishermen and bairns who had braved the elements in the hope of finding their loved ones paced the shore line, dismissive of the huge breakers roaring in, helpless despite the desperate cries. Women stricken with grief, carrying wailing bairns and burdened with children clutching their skirts, crying in unison. Unable to understand what was happening they cried because everyone else cried. One or two of the mothers could not bear the sight and walked slowly home to deal with their sorrow alone.

Lenny was devastated that all his crew, one of them being Billy who had substituted for him at the last minute, husband of one night, was lost along with their newly built boat. They were so proud of this brand new rig built at great financial cost and manpower by four brothers now smashed to smithereens and floating like matchsticks on the angry sea. Lenny tried desperately to push through the wind and the blinding spray on the slippery rocks to reach those calling for help. Emotionally deeply hurt he tried to make amends but to no avail. Lenny was overwrought. In his heart he knew but for fate he should have gone down with his crew. He wondered how he would ever come to terms with such a situation but he had done what he felt was right at the time.

In the aftermath of this storm, there were seventy eight widows and numerous fatherless children. Bodies were washed ashore and had to be buried. Many unidentified body parts were interred in a mass grave on Fort point. How were all these families who had lost their main bread winner going to be fed? It was indeed a tragic loss for the whole community. A stifled cry of excitement could be heard when later some who had ridden ahead of the storm managed to reach home.

Some months on, Mary, now with another child but without a husband, once again, stoically returned to her old life with her parents. They looked after the children, cooking and making rag rugs in the evenings while Mary continued to collect mussels to bait the lines. Lenny helped the family whenever he could. Sometimes on a Sunday afternoon he would walk with Mary to place flowers on the mass grave in remembrance of Billy and all those who had lost their lives. Mary gradually came to terms with her grief, as did many others. Such are the vicissitudes of life.

The following June the sombre mood in Eyemouth lifted for a day. The wedding bells rang out for the wedding of Lenny and Mary. The now decimated community put its grief on hold for a day. Everyone was determined to make it a happy time for the newly wed couple and enjoyed the celebrations. Lenny made a sincere and loyal husband. He worked hard to help raise the family that Billy was denied. Such is the fickle finger of fate.

This story is set against an historical catastrophe. It does not claim to be an accurate account of the event. The story and characters are fictitious.

Refs:

1 Eyemouth Museum
2 'Black Friday', The Eyemouth Fishing Disaster 1881. Peter Aitchison

JUST A LINE

By Peter Zentler-Munro

You can't see it, feel it, touch it, smell it or hear it but it's there all right – an invisible border that is represented only by a line drawn on a map. It's a line that divides families, imposes rules and taxes that are different, perhaps only a few feet away on the other side. Apart from those born in the Borders, for whom the real border begins ten or twenty miles away on either side of that almost imaginary line defining the border between Scotland and England; for the British, borders and frontiers take on almost mystical significance.

In 1970s western Europe, it was very different, nobody bothered very much. If you lived in, for example, Hamburg, Frankfurt (either of them), or Berlin, you were first a Hamburger, Frankfurter or Berliner, and a long way second, a German. In 1976, I went to stay with Karl in Saarbrucken, a guy I met in the Madrid youth hostel, the previous year. Karl had degrees in French, Spanish, Russian and Economics, and an estranged wife, because he couldn't manage to hold down a job. Not because of drugs or drunkenness, he just couldn't get interested. Instead, he went to auctions, bought bargain lots and sold items on a Saturday market stall.

'Today', he announced after breakfast on my first morning in Germany, 'we are walking across the border to go shopping. 'Bring your passport, just in case. As I live here in the frontier zone, I can't buy anything in the frontier zone of France without paying tax at the German border, therefore, if we're stopped you have to say you bought everything.'

'So, how can we buy anything?' I asked, innocently.

'It's different for you, you can buy anything, food for travel, gifts, things to take home to Scotland, you've got a British passport, and foreign visitors pay no tax.'

The first town in France was an hour's walk away, along a single-track road, through fields of waving corn and across a river on a rickety wooden bridge. It was a hot day, and I needed a rest. 'How long before we get to France?'

'We're in France already; we crossed the border half an hour ago— see that church spire – that's where we're going.'

'I didn't see any border.'

'They very rarely patrol this road but they could do; we'll go back a different way, just in case.'

Karl spent 800 francs (about £75) in three shops, though he paid in marks and got change in francs. We stored the purchases — perfume, brandy, toilet water in our day sacks and returned, stopping for lunch at a café where Karl evidently knew the family. I looked in a junk shop and emerged with a small collection of Channel Islands stamps, perhaps stolen by an occupying German soldier. We saw no patrol on our return, either.

Next day, he drove me into the city of Metz along the main road. In those pre-Schengen days, the border posts were sometimes wooden huts, as they were that day, or brick buildings, situated about 150 metres apart. Going into France, we were waved through the German control and stopped by the French. My passport was inspected and stamped, Karl's was ignored. After an exhausting trek around Metz looking at the cathedral, the basilica and several museums, eating a spicy Arabic lunch and a fruity Indian curry for dinner, we returned. The gendarmes at the French control exchanged pleasantries but did not ask for passports, the German control not only asked for passports but asked to look in the back of the van and were obviously astonished to see it was empty.

'You see the problem?' asked Karl.

'Not really. We had a great day, thank you. We didn't buy anything.'

'The problem is that I can't buy antiques in France and sell them in Germany, at least not without paying tax.'

'But you're making a profit from the market stall, aren't you?'

'I am but it's not enough.'

He stopped the van and parked about 300 metres from his flat. 'It's a bit of a walk but the near spaces will all be taken.' We dawdled along the road and I saw that, indeed, there were no empty parking spaces.

I made coffee when we got in.

'You said you weren't making enough profit ...' I began, 'are you selling too cheaply, or paying too much?'

'The percentage profit is OK; it's rather that I can't sell enough on my stall to have an adequate standard of living. It takes the same amount of effort to sell jewellery for 100 marks as it does to sell a bit of furniture for 500 marks.'

'What are the constraints?'

'My market stall isn't big enough, even if I could get another pitch, it wouldn't be adjacent. I don't have the capital to rent a shop, and actually I can't buy much furniture in the auctions here; the prices are too steep.

'Is furniture cheaper in France, then?'

'Much cheaper, especially Second Empire stuff. The French are into modernity.'

I thought for a moment. 'Second Empire, is that Napoleon III?' Karl nodded, 'So, Second Empire is roughly 1850 to 1870 – mid-Victorian?'

He nodded again. 'It's all the rage, here. Well, perhaps not here exactly, but in the cities further north'. The phone rang. Karl listened, said 'But ... but ... no ... yes, Mother ... bye'. He put the receiver down, sat down, drank half his mug and said 'Damn. That's torn it. That was Mum, reminding me it's Granny's birthday on Sunday.'

'Oh, what's she like?'

'Terrifying, or at least she was when I was growing up. Now, she's slowed down a bit, she's terrifying but nice. She's got a list of things for me to do before the party.'

'Like what?' I asked, intrigued.

'Split logs, remove cobwebs, change light bulbs, move furniture, hang curtains, probably lots more. Thing is, I've got to get my van TUV (the German MOT) tomorrow and then get her a present. You'll also find she yacks all the time, whether there's anyone listening or not.'

'Why don't you take me round there, I'll do some chores, and you can go off and collect me later. I've got nothing better to do.'

'Would you really? There's no need to stay long. There's a bus stop outside her door and the bus goes right past here.'

'That sounds like a plan, what time do we need to leave?'

'If we leave here at nine am, I'll have time for a coffee before the TUV. I'll ring you at Granny's house tomorrow, if I am going to be long delayed.'

Karl was up long before me, preparing his van for the TUV. In Germany, it was widely believed that a van could fail if it was dirty, untidy or didn't have all the paperwork for replacement parts.

We set out before nine. I was amazed to find his Granny lived only ten minutes away.

We were both greeted with kisses on both cheeks, in the French fashion. Karl's granny was a short woman in her sixties. Her lined face, topped by white hair, was at odds with her slim unwrinkled arms and legs. She wore a translucent green top, by which I mean that I could see her bra constraining her breasts underneath, a short patterned skirt, white ankle socks and sandals. She said 'Karl, how nice to see you, why don't you come more often?' Turning to me, she continued 'You must call me Grandmère, I'm enchanted to make your acquaintance.'

She spoke in French, to my surprise. 'I'll make some coffee'.

'Why is she speaking French?'

'Although she was born in Germany, she is an ardent Francophile,' he whispered,'she prefers speaking French. Look at the furniture, the paintings, the crockery – it's all French.'

She came in at that point. 'I was born here in this house and I hope to die here. When I was born, it was in Germany, but while I was growing up it was in France. In the thirties, it became Germany again. After the war, it was French again, and now it's back in Germany.'

'That's interesting,' I said. We drank coffee and ate coconut biscuits and had a bit of general chitchat.

Karl began, 'Mum has told me you want some help. I've got to deliver my van for the TUV this morning but Peter has volunteered to take my place until I return.'

65

'But he's on holiday!'

'Well, I am, but I've nothing better to do and if it helps you or Karl, that's OK. What would you like me to do?'

'Visit all the rooms and sweep away the cobwebs. I'd like to wash the curtains in the downstairs rooms, so if you could take them down that would be great. While you've got the ladder there, perhaps you could put new light-bulbs in the sockets, it would be a nuisance if a bulb went during the party. I want to use the blue crockery but it needs to be rinsed …'

Karl interrupted, 'Grandmère, I have to go now.'

'OK, see you later, drive safely.'

'Bye!' he said as he left.

'Where is the ladder, please?'

'It's outside, next to an apple tree, I'll show you.'

The ladder was jointed and it took all my strength to carry it through to the salon, and then I saw a young woman standing there. Grandmère introduced me, 'This is Peter, a friend of my grandson's, and this is Maria, who does my cleaning and shopping.' Maria was a few years older than me and incredibly beautiful. Taller than Grandmère, her waist-length black hair made her seem almost as tall as me, brown eyes, and a snub nose. She was wearing a pink smock over a blouse, open at the top. A mini-skirt, socks and plain brown shoes completed my assessment.

The ceiling seemed a long way up. Maria unfolded the ladder and set it up in front of the window and said 'I'll hold the ladder steady while you go up'. I climbed and found the curtains were now in easy reach. 'You have a good view, don't you?' was her ambiguous comment. I agreed, trying not to look down on her cleavage. I unhooked the curtains and came down. I moved the ladder under the light. 'First, help me to take the hooks out of the curtains so that Frau Schlossmacher can wash them.' I followed her lead and took the hookless curtains into the utility room.

'Will the curtains dry in time for your party, Grandmère?'

'In this heat, certainly.'

Maria and I did the other two rooms, by which time the other curtains had been washed.

'Where is the blue crockery, please?' I asked Maria.

She knelt by a low cupboard in the kitchen and gradually handed it up to me; I piled it up on top of the dresser. Our fingers kept on touching. When she finished, she staggered as she got up. I put out my hands to stop her falling and somehow found I was holding her waist. That was a shared moment which I evaded, merely saying 'Thank you'.

While I did the cobwebs and washed and dried the crockery, Grandmère washed more curtains and hung them out, Maria dusted, hoovered and cleaned.

As I dried the last plate, Maria came in and said, 'It's time for lunch.'

66

There was salad, cheese and crusty rolls and white wine.

'Is this German wine?' I asked Grandmère.

'Yes, but it's French lettuce, tomatoes, peppers, onions and mushrooms.'

'How do you know?'

'It's all from the garden.'

'I thought we were in Germany?'

'We are, but most of the garden is in France. Maria, would you show Peter the garden after lunch while I have my snooze?' Turning to me, she said, 'There's a path at the bottom through a wood that goes to the main road.'

Maria led me through the garden, and as we passed a gooseberry hedge, she said 'This is the frontier, now we are in France. We walked past lettuce, tomatoes, chives, walnut trees before I realised we had crossed the line between familiarity and intimacy and were holding hands. In the sun, we kissed, then walked another forty yards to the bottom of the garden. I saw a large shed, seemingly empty. We walked into the wood, snogging and cuddling. The track to the road was about half a mile, and as we exited the wood, I saw a junction with a signpost 'Allemagne 2' and on the other arms, other destinations.

By the time we got back, Grandmère had had her snooze, the curtains were dry, so Maria and I rehung them. 'Karl phoned, he's not coming, the van needs to be repaired.' Turning to Maria, Grandmère said 'Would you take Peter back, please?' I spent the night at Maria's before she took me back.

The party was fun and I danced with Maria when she wasn't serving drinks or food, and I went back to Maria's, to Karl's amusement.

I met Karl mid-morning and asked 'When's the next auction in France?'

'There's one in Forbach, tomorrow. Why?'

'I've worked out how to get your purchases across the border, without paying tax.'

'Really? How?'

'Did you know that half of Grandmère's garden is in France?'

'I didn't. I know her house is near the frontier but I didn't realise it was that near.'

'Maria and I walked down a track from the garden onto the main road in France. If I'm right, you could drive from the auction up the track, pop your purchases into the shed and transport them up the garden, through the house and they're in Germany.'

He rang Grandmère and explained my idea. 'She's happy with the idea. The key is hanging on a nail by the shed door and she says there's a trolley inside the shed.'

'Well, let's go and try.' We found the track easily enough, and although it was a bit soft in places, we got the van up without any problem. We found the key, and saw the trolley. One of the tyres was punctured.

'That'll be easily fixed. If you help me get in the van, we can take it to a garage.'

'Let's go and view the auction.'

The following day, Karl bought lots of old furniture for a song. Some of it needed a bit of loving care and he arranged to collect it, two days later, after the auction had cashed his cheque.

We picked up the trolley, delivered it to the shed and went and had tea with Grandmère.

CONTRIBUTORS

Susan Allen's writing career began when she wrote a poem on a Buddhist Retreat in 2008. By 2016 she'd written her first novel, **A Mosaic in Time**. Her readers requested a sequel. **The Mosaic Morphs** will be available Winter 2021. Weathered, wiser, and happier, Susan now lives and writes in the Scottish Borders. susanlallenauthor.com

Rosalyn M Anderson - After writing for clinical texts before retirement, I am aiming for a family memoir with fictionalisation! As well as anthology contributions and research pieces published for The Wilson's Tales Project, Heavy Horse magazine recently accepted an item about family artefacts so my memoir journey has started!

Antoine d'Y Bisset - Born some time ago in a fishing village, I have worked for various businesses in management and sales. Sold champagne to HM the Queen at Buckingham Palace and carrots to Balmoral; sold smoked salmon to the Elysee Palace and cream cakes to IBM. I have retired from this.

Hayley Emberey - The Scottish Borders is the perfect place for Hayley to complete her series of five audio children's stories 'Magical Realism'. Hayley is working on her first novel 'The Scent' due out in 2022, based on a true story, a supernatural psychological thriller/love story with a film script in the pipeline.

Michael A Fenty - I am a retired GP Throughout my working life, I contributed articles to various journals and had a column in Scottish Medicine. After retirement, I had plays The Resurrection Man and Fracked produced. In 2016 I wrote Tibbie Tamson produced for the BYT by Judy Steel.

Vee Freir is a retired Clinical Psychologist, who took up writing after moving to the Borders in 2008. She has written non-fiction books, poems, short stories and a play. Her last book 'Learn To Stress Less: 50 Simple and Effective Tips for a Stress-Free Life' can be found on Amazon.

Pamela Gordon wrote many policy reports during her career in local government but when she retired she indulged her ambition to write historical fiction. She's published a series of six stories set in the 15th century and some short stories. A novel set in 19th century Sheffield is due out soon.

Michael Hutchinson - After studying Fine Art, Michael turned to writing, working in different forms including script, feature, and fiction. His script, Jericho, was produced by post-graduates at the Northern Film School, Leeds, and he's had features published in several UK magazines. Michael is currently working on a collection of short stories.

Anita John is a published poet and playwright and runs wildlife writing workshops for RSPB Scotland Loch Leven. Her poem 'Sixteen' was recently Highly Commended in the Gerard Rochford Poetry Prize 2021 and her poem 'Voices' shortlisted in the Bridport Prize 2021. More of her work can be found at anitajohn.co.uk/

Elisabeth Kelly has had her poems published in a number of anthologies and in print and online journals. She has a slim pamphlet published by HydridDreich, a pamphlet due out 2021 with Hedgehog Poetry Press and a memoir/poetry chapbook due out early 2022 with Selcouth Station. She tweets @eekelly22.

Jane Pearn is currently chair of Borders Writer's Forum. She writes mostly poetry and short stories, which have appeared in several online and print magazines. She has two published poetry collections and has recently been working on a commissioned poem to mark Sir Walter Scott's 250th anniversary.

Cate L Ryan is a visual artist & musician. Began writing while travelling around Crete with late husband and soul-mate, Rin. Returning, an incident on a 19A bus sparked a story, then more … . Inspiration is music, wild walks in the hills. Themes of transformation, renewal, myth, memory; the lost and found. www.spanglefish.com/catelryan

Barbara Usher has taught in both mainstream and special needs schools. Since moving to the Borders in 2017, she teaches students with complex needs. With her husband Martin, and dogs, Noah and Joshua, she has developed a smallholding and animal sanctuary from their four acres.

Patricia Watts moved to the Scottish Borders nine years ago where she joined the Borders Writers' Forum and the Kelso Writers. She writes short stories for adults and children. She has completed a children's book and her first adult novel is ready for publication. Patricia is now a member of Silver Quill

Peter Zentler-Munro - I've been writing a family and local history column in the Border Telegraph and Peeblesshire News for over twelve years. Two years after I started, Kelso Writers and Borders Writers' Forum inspired me to start writing and publishing short stories. I've also written a thirty minute play.

AIMS

- To promote interest and raise the profile of contemporary local writers

- To provide a focus for writing-related events in the Scottish Borders

- To provide networking opportunities

- To support professional development through talks, regular readings and workshops

- To offer fellow writers a friendly and supportive environment

Further details, including a programme of events available on www.borderswritersforum.org.uk

Printed in Great Britain
by Amazon